FINDING
a Soulful Love

LUCINDA JOHNSON

STRATTON
—PRESS—
Publishing Life

Finding A Soulful Love
Copyright © 2021 **Lucinda Johnson**

Stratton Press Publishing
831 N Tatnall Street Suite M #188,
Wilmington, DE 19801
www.stratton-press.com
1-888-323-7009

ISBN (Paperback): 978-1-64895-429-0
ISBN (Hardback): 978-1-64895-430-6
ISBN (Ebook): 978-1-64895-433-7

Printed in the United States of America

Dedication

I would like to dedicate this novel to my One True Love for giving me the inspiration to write. It all began with the fantasies and poems I would write for you. You came into my world and brough with you so much joy and happiness to our journey. Always-Only-You, AKF.

Acknowledgements

I would like to give thanks to God for blessing me with the talent to write this novel. All Praise Belongs To God.

To Reggie and Ronnie my beloved boys, thanks for believing that I could do this. I love you with all my heart.

Thanks to my friends who enjoyed reading my drafts. Latoya, thank you for the photo and poem you created that was based on inserts from my novel.

A special thanks to my editors and production team.

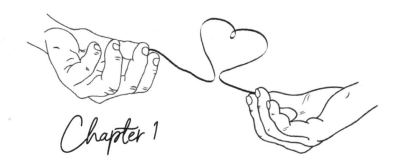

Chapter 1

My name is Cynthia, and I have gone through several changes in my life. I was raised by my grandmother, Lucille, who I thought was my mother until her death. It all began with my leaving Florida and moving to Philadelphia, which was the City of Brotherly Love and Sisterly Affection.

During my time in Florida, I had what I thought was a peaceful upbringing. My family consisted of two aunts, six cousins (three girls and three boys), and Mom.

Of all the cousins, Debra Mayhue and I were the closest. Maybe we were the closest because we were the youngest of the cousins, and our birthdays were the same, except we were a year apart. Of the other cousins, four were actually sisters and brothers, and Aunt Glady was their mom. Aunt Janice and her son mostly kept to themselves on what I called the west wing of the house. Mom took care of Debra and me.

The house I grew up in was enormous with a lot of land around it. In my eyes, it was a mansion. It had five bedrooms, a den, a foyer, two bathrooms, a combined living room and dining room area, and a large closed-in porch. There was a park behind my house that gave me an extended backyard. There was even a pecan tree in the backyard that I enjoyed climbing every day. Yes, there was a little tomboy in me (as the saying goes). Mom always yelled at me for being in that tree. "I'm raising a girl, not a boy!" Mom would say.

The weather was hot during the day, and then it settled into a cool summer night's breeze, where all that was needed was a lightweight jacket.

My mom and I would sit on the back steps to watch whatever seasonal sports were played at the park. She would make hot dogs and cherry Kool-Aid for us. Whether it was hockey, football, or basketball, we always cheered for opposite teams.

Mom would say, "Cynthia, what's the fun in cheering for the same team? We need to create some competition. Healthy competition is always a good thing."

Football was, of course, Mom's favorite sport, being that her husband was an avid player. I never knew him, and actually, there were never any males who participated in my upbringing. Of all the sports Mom and I watched, soccer was the one I didn't care for very much.

When the game was over, Mom would let Debra and I go to the park and gather up the empty soda and beer bottles from underneath the bleachers and throughout the park. Debra didn't like sports, but she wanted to reap the benefits from the sale of the empty bottles. We would sell the bottles to the neighborhood junkyard dealer, Mr. Stevenson, who we called Mr. Necktie, for two cents each. Mr. Stevenson got that name because no matter what he had on, there was always a tie around his neck, even when he had on a sweat suit (his trademark, shall we say).

He lived at the end of the block, so his home didn't take away from the value of the development. All his junk was in a very large shed that he built in his backyard after several complaints from the neighbors. In the next block was the supermarket, and across the street from it Mr. Smith's Steak Shop, which is where we would buy curly fries and penny candy for our tea party. When we got home, we set things up on the front porch and got our doll babies and cherry Kool-Aid that Mom made as our choice of beverage.

Mom sat on the porch across from us and read her Bible with a cup of tea. My other cousins would be running around in the yard or at the park. The other girl cousins didn't like tea parties. They thought tea parties with doll babies were dumb, yet they had imaginary friends.

For the most part, everyone was happy until the visitors from hell came, and we all had to deal with them. The hell came with the four cousins who visited every summer, which Mom took responsibility for (Kevin, George, Patricia, and Denise). They were sisters and brothers and lived in Philadelphia with their mom, Brenda Watson. She was Mom's oldest child. She left to pursue a career in education. Brenda had seven kids, but only the four youngest came to visit. They didn't really fit into our surroundings, so we couldn't wait until they went back home. The youngest of the four cousins was Kevin; he was a year younger than me. He picked on me a lot, which caused us to fight during his visit. Patricia was bossy, Denise was motherly, and George, well, he was quiet. George was the only one I liked. When they were there, the focus was on making them happy, no matter how miserable they were making us. Mom would also get into arguments with my aunts about them picking on their kids.

Debra and I felt ignored by Mom, so when we expressed how we felt, Mom just said, "Be patient, my girls, they will be going home soon." When they left, we had a pizza party to celebrate.

The unity was back—well, at least until William Brown came along. He was the new boy on the block, and we both wanted him. He was the one reason Debra and I didn't get along. William and his family moved onto the block shortly after the new year began (1970). Since William and I attended the same school (Mary McCloud Bethune Junior High), we sat next to each other on the bus. We would talk about the kids, as they got on the bus, from the other neighborhoods.

One day during English class, William walked over to where I was sitting and asked me if I wanted to be his girlfriend. I said yes. When I got home and told Debra, she didn't speak to me for a week. Mom made us start talking to each other again. Well, actually, the threat of an ass whopping from Mom is what really did it.

William started carrying my books when he would walk me to my classes. It was also cute the way he always kissed me on the forehead when we separated from each other. When we weren't at school, we hung out at the park or on each other's porch. That was pretty much it for twelve-year-old kids in love.

William was the first boy I ever kissed with my tongue; that is French-kissed. It was out in the shed we had in the backyard. I will never forget that kiss because that was also the first time Mom gave me an ass whopping. Yes, my mom caught us. We were so engrossed in that kiss that I didn't even hear her when she came into the shed. I just felt a tap on my shoulder and a voice, with an angry tone, that said, "Cynthia, get your behind in the house, and, William, I will speak with your mother soon. Now get on home."

William ran out that shed like a bat out of hell. I ran in the house and waited for Mom, knowing that it was going to be trouble. When she came in, she sent me back outside to get her three good switches. Yep, I was getting a southern ass whopping. I gave her the switches, and she made me sit in a chair while she sat on the bed to plait them together.

The tears were rolling down my face when she asked, "Have I hit you?"

"No, but you will," was my response as I watched her continue to plait those switches.

"Get your fast behind over here," she said as she got up from the bed.

"But, Mom…"

Before I could say anything else, I felt the switch on my body. Words were coming out her mouth, but I don't remember what they were. I was too busy crying and trying to get away to hear what she was saying.

When she was done, she had me sit back in that chair, and I got the full lecture on the do's and don'ts of being with a boy.

A few days later, Mom told me we were going away for a while. I was thirteen, and this would be my first trip away from home. I should have been excited, but I wasn't because I didn't want to go anywhere that meant leaving my cousin Debra and especially my boyfriend William.

Then I figured the reason we were leaving had to do with me kissing William. Mom would keep me away from him for the rest of the summer, and we would be back when school started in the fall. Little did I know!

Once we left and arrived in Philadelphia, I found out several hours later that this was going to be my permanent home. That it was my mom's illness that took us away to live with my cousins from hell.

Everything I knew changed. The peace and serenity of that southern life was snatched away via that airplane flight to Philadelphia. Debra and William were lost to me forever. There was this song, I cannot remember the artist, but it had the words "I found love on a two-way street and lost it on a lonely highway." This made me think of William every time I heard it. He stayed in my heart for quite some time.

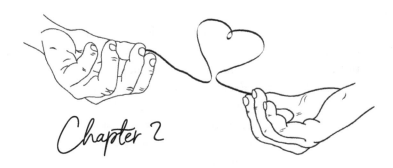

Chapter 2

Now my new family included five brothers and three sisters. Some of them I knew, and the others, who were older, I didn't know. In other words, this was when I learned that four out of the eight were my sisters and brothers and not my cousins, as I once believed. Yes, they were the visiting cousins from hell. With the exception of the two oldest kids, we were all going to be living in this house (situated in the heart of north Philadelphia). One of them was a sister, who had her own apartment, and the other a brother, who was in the army. He was married, and his wife had an apartment on a nearby street.

I remembered my first conversation with the woman of the house the day we arrived. It was a three-story house with a basement. We went into a bedroom that was off to the right, at the top of the stairs, on the second floor. The room had a twin bed, a four-drawer dresser that a

TV sat on, and a closet where the door stood opened. I remembered thinking I wished I could go in there, close the door, and wait for Mom to come and get me and take me back to Florida. Even better, I could close my eyes just to open them and realize that this was all a bad dream.

This short lady who was a little stocky—and with a mean look on her face to boot—walked over to the window and called me over to where she was standing. "Come here, Cynthia," she said.

I wouldn't, or shall I say, couldn't move closer to her. I had frozen near the door where I was standing. I could hear her voice, but I couldn't move. Therefore, she called me again.

"Cynthia, come over here, now!"

Being that I heard a different tone in her voice from the first time she called me, I walked over and stood beside her with fear running through my veins. Standing in front of the window, which looked out into an alleyway, she said, "My name is Barbara, and I'm your mother." Yes, this was the Barbara I thought was my aunt. Mom's oldest daughter.

"No, you're not. My mom is upstairs, and she's sick," I said as my eyes began to tear up, and I tried to walk away.

She grabbed my arm and said, "That, Cynthia, is your grandmother, and she is dying of cancer. You'll be living here now, and you'll call my husband Dad. Is that understood?" She said this with a tone that said I had better answer with an understanding to what she said.

All I could say was yes. Even if I didn't understand what was going on, she was scary enough for me to say whatever it was that she wanted to hear. Then I ran out the room and upstairs to the woman who was now known to me as my grandmother. I dropped to my knees at the side of her bed and just kept saying, "Don't leave me, Mom, please don't leave me. I don't know these people, and I want to go home. Please take me home."

"I'm sorry, Cindy, but I had to bring you here. You belong with your mother now. I should have explained all of this to you before we left Florida. I thought your mother and I would tell you everything together."

"She's not my mom. You are." Tears continued to run down my face. "I'm your daughter. I don't care what she told me. You don't have to leave me with these people. My aunts at home will take care of me. Let's go home. They will take care of us. Please, Mom, let's go back home."

Barbara came upstairs after me. She pulled me up from where I was bending at my grandma's bedside. She pulled me into her arms and tried to comfort me.

"Let me go!" I cried out and pulled away. "I was lied to my entire life. Don't touch me. You didn't want me. If Grandma wasn't sick, I wouldn't be here. I have cousins who are now my sisters and brothers. I hate you, I hate you!" I ran downstairs and went back into that room until my grandmother came down to me. She held me for what seemed like hours.

I sat at my grandma's bedside during the day and slept next to her every night. She would talk to me about life and things she thought I might go through as I got older. No one bothered me during this time. I only left her long enough to eat and change my clothes. Barbara wouldn't let me eat in the bedroom.

I could see the life draining from her, so I decided not to upset her with any more talk about going home, and I stopped crying in front of her. When I talked to one of my aunts about what had happened, she just said, "I understand how you feel, but you need to let her live in peace with whatever time she has left."

My grandma died a month later. Just because I had to call her Grandma for a month because I was told to, in my heart, she will always be Mom.

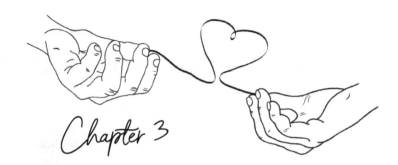

Chapter 3

Like I said, growing up with my family down south, there was peace, and in this new environment, the uncertainty of it made me miserable. It became chaotic because everything I knew was changing, and I had no say at all. I became the "Cinderella" of the family, and everyone's chores became mine.

I remembered when my sister, Patricia (the sister formerly known as Patricia, the mean visiting cousin from hell), said to me, "You're going to do the dishes on my days, and if you tell Mom, I'll kick your ass." She had that same mean look Barbara had the first time I met her. At least my sister Denise (the nice summer cousin who was trying to make me feel a little comfortable) just made me do her chores without the threats. It didn't matter either way because I wasn't going to tell. I wasn't sure what Barbara would say and didn't want to make things any worse than they already were.

As time moved on, there was never a bond with Barbara or my sisters and brothers. I still couldn't understand, even to this day, how Barbara could desert me. I'm sure that holding on to these feelings kept me from getting close to this family. Of course, they weren't trying to get close to me either.

I felt that this was the most selfish thing a mother could do. How could a mother raise all but one of her children? Sure, parents gave their children to family members all the time. This was no new thing in that it was happening with me, but they generally gave all of them away, spreading them throughout the family.

I just couldn't understand how Barbara could take six kids with her and never send for her seventh child. Then a year later, she would have another son, and still no desire to come for the daughter she left down south. Even worse, when she did have to take her daughter, still probably not by her choice, there was yet another son who was six months old. All I knew was that I wasn't going to do this to my children.

How did I keep from going into a state of depression with the way I was feeling and being treated? Well, all I can say is, "Thank God for the girl who lived two doors down from me." Her name was Teresa Andrews. Teresa lived with her much older sister. Her mom passed away when she was ten years old. She was tall, light skinned, and full of life. Being raised by her older sister, she was glad to be with someone her own age and someone to get in trouble with. In time, we became the best of friends. In fact, we became more like sisters. We were always together,

Cynthia and Teresa, two peas in a pod. I could talk to her about anything.

Being at her house was always better than being at my house. When we had our talks, I told her about how I wish I could go back to that peaceful life I had in Florida instead of being here feeling angry and bitter. There would be times when we talked that tears would roll down her face from the emotions that took control of my feelings. We would cry together, and she would pull me closer to her and place my head on her shoulder. Teresa was a very passionate person.

After my grandma's death, Teresa was the only other person who I felt gave me love. It was an instant connection between us. She wanted nothing from me and was there whenever I needed her.

Once, during one of our many conversations, I asked Teresa, with tears running down my face, "Do you think I would be here if my grandma never got sick? Why, damn it? Why didn't Barbara want me?"

"You know, Cynthia, you can't dwell on that now," she said as she wiped the tears from my eyes.

"I know, Teresa, but I still can't help wondering about it. What would have happened if my aunts kept me? Would I have ever been told that I had a mother, three sisters, and five brothers who lived in Philadelphia, and that it was my grandma who raised me?"

"I don't think you will ever know the answer to these questions," Teresa replied. "Anyway, it's Friday. Go fix your face, and let's go hang out down South Philly with the gang." Teresa had introduced me to all of her friends.

Off we went, and we had a very good time. The only thing that spoiled that night was the punishment we got for missing curfew. It was for a week, and we couldn't spend any time together. The curfew law was 9:00 p.m. for kids under sixteen. The last time we missed curfew, we could at least hang out on the block. I think this punishment was harder because this time the police were involved.

When we came up from the subway, there was a police officer standing there. We tried to run back down the steps, hoping he didn't see us, but he blew his whistle, and we knew we were caught. He drove us home and, before leaving, gave us tickets. Anyway, we were usually more alert when we knew we broke curfew. It was just that we had so much fun that we were still talking about it when we got off the train. We weren't on our curfew game. To tell the truth, we were a little tipsy from a bottle of red wine that we shared with one of our older friends.

Things moved along for a while before Teresa and I talked about Barbara again. I was trying to let it go, just focusing on being a teenager who had school, chores, and homework to deal with.

Then one night after washing dishes, my brother Kevin (that other so-called cousin from hell that I spent summers fighting with) decided he wanted to tease me. He started chanting, "Mama doesn't love you, and Mama doesn't love you." I got so mad that I pushed him away from me and went to Teresa's house. After I got myself together, we started watching a movie, which I liked until this one scene brought tears to my eyes. It was about a woman who just found out about her adoption. She tracked her mother down, and after finding out the reason why her mother left her, the mother apologized for leaving. They went on to have a nice mother-daughter relationship.

I looked over at Teresa and said, "I wish my mother would say I'm sorry for not being there. Sometimes that's all a child wants to hear when they're being reconnected with a parent."

"Girl, I can, in a way, feel your pain, even though I haven't experienced what you're going through. Call it friendship pain," Teresa said with a smile on her face.

I didn't think so, but it was sweet of her to say it. Especially when my next question to her was, "Teresa, if my own mother never loved me, do you think anyone ever will?" There was still no bonding with any members of my family, and I hadn't heard from anyone in Florida. It was as if they forgot I existed.

"Yes, Cynthia, someone will love you. I love you," said Teresa as she got up, walked over, and pulled me up for a hug. Teresa spent a lot of time hugging me. I knew it was her way of trying to give me the affection I wasn't getting at home. She knew just how I felt about my household.

I didn't belong in that house, and it surely didn't help when my brothers and sisters continued to remind me that Barbara didn't want me. I wouldn't argue with them; I would just go to my bedroom and cry. This situation was still hard for me to deal with no matter how hard I tried to let it go.

Every time I wanted to tell Barbara how I was feeling, I couldn't bring myself to do it. Maybe seeing me again had just as much of an effect on her as it did for me. I took to reading the Bible as a means of getting some peace of mind. I read from the book of Psalms. Psalm 23 and Psalm 121 were my favorites because they were the chapters that my grandma always read to Debra and me.

Every day for the next six months, before going to bed, I would say, "Cynthia, this is your family. The surroundings are different, but you need to learn to adapt. It's what Grandma would have wanted. That's why she brought you here." I even tried to convince myself that my aunts wanted me to stay in Florida, but they couldn't talk my grandma into letting them raise me. I guess she felt it was time for Barbara to take responsibility for me.

Teresa was a good friend, like a sister, and I knew she loved me, but it wasn't her love that I was reaching out for now. I was beginning to want for someone who could hold me and make things better in a relationship way. I could have a family where I belonged. So I started dating and met who I thought was a wonderful man. I met him at Teresa's house, at her sixteenth birthday party. I walked in, and there he was, standing in her dining room looking so damn fine. He was about 5'5" tall and bowlegged. He was dressed in a red cashmere sweater and blue jeans.

I walked up to him and asked, "What's your name? I've spent a lot of time over here, and I don't remember ever seeing you."

"It's Randall Jones, and what's yours?" he replied.

"Cynthia, but my closest friends call me Cindy. Well, except for Teresa. She likes calling me by my full name. So, where's Teresa?" It was time to go and get the scoop on Randall.

"She's in the kitchen with my brother."

"Okay. I'll be talking to you real soon."

He smiled at me and that gave me a good vibe. I was going to get to know this man. I walked away hoping he was checking me out. I looked back, and he was. Yes! All I could do was smile.

I needed some details about this man, but Teresa was talking to someone, so I had to wait. She was on her way out, but not before I had a chance to whisper in her ear, "I want to know about the good-looking bowlegged man named Randall."

"I'll talk to you about him tomorrow. I got a date," she whispered back into my ear.

Randall and I just looked at each other and smiled. I watched him walk out the door following behind Teresa and his brother.

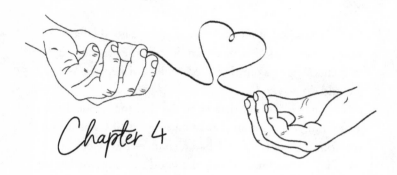

Chapter 4

On the way to school that morning, I got the lowdown on Randall. He was a year younger, had two sisters, and of course a brother. A few more details, then Teresa said, "I'm going to see Jesse after school. If you want to come with me, you can."

"Try and stop me. I want to go and meet Randall because he is going to be my baby's daddy. Little Randall Jr. will know his mother as Mom and his grandmother as Grandma. So is Jesse the man you left with yesterday?"

"Yes. Like you, I met him at the party. He's Randall's brother. They came with my brother Bernard."

"I didn't know you had a brother. You never talked about him."

"He's my older half brother. We don't really talk that much. He grew up with his father. It's a long—"

Before she could finish what she was saying, I stopped her and said, "Forget about him and tell me about Jesse."

"Well, he's going to be my baby's daddy. He's a smooth talker and a fast mover. That's why I didn't get a chance to tell you about him at the party. Before I knew it, we were on our way to the movies. That was his birthday present to me. I told him we could go tomorrow, but he wanted to go last night. I asked my mom, and she said it was okay."

Once we reached school, the conversation ended until we met at lunch. On the way home from school, we talked about the life we were going to have with them. We were going to marry them and live in a mansion. Once we got home, the plan was to meet back up at seven that night so that we could go see Jesse and Randall.

When we got there, Teresa knocked on the door, and a girl let us in. It was one of their sisters. Randall and Jesse were sitting on the sofa in the living room. Randall was looking good, and when he looked at me, all I could do was smile. Jesse got up to hug Teresa, and I sat down next to Randall. Teresa and Jesse went down in the basement while Randall and I stayed in the living room. We spent the evening telling each other everything we could about us. We talked so much that Randall went into the kitchen to get us something to drink. He had commented on the fact that his mouth was getting dry from all the talking.

I didn't see Teresa again until it was time to go home. Before I left, he gave me a good night kiss. He pulled me into his arms, and before I knew it, he had his tongue down my throat. Wow! My second French kiss. I didn't want to leave from his arms. As I recall that night, Teresa had to pull me away from him.

After our first hookup, we saw each other just about every day. We did many things together. We went to the movies, concerts, we hung out with friends, and spent time being alone down in his mother's basement. I'm sure I don't need to say what went on in the basement. What I can say is that I was the first to initiate sex. It went something like "It's hot down here. Do you mind if I take my shirt off?" I can't remember if I waited for an answer, but the shirt was on the floor, and, well, it was on. Our hands were all over each other's body as we examine the parts of our bodies that excited us the most. Once our bodies connected and he put his lips on my breast, the moaning and groaning began. We knew this would happen over and over again. It felt good. I couldn't wait to tell Teresa that we did it.

We had been seeing each other for a year, so we made plans to get together and celebrate our anniversary. We went to McDonald's. Hey, we were teenagers! What do you expect?

"Happy anniversary, Cindy," Randall said as he gave me a card.

"Thank you, Randall," I replied as I gave him my card. We started talking about how we were going to get married after college and move to Florida to raise our family.

"We are going to have two boys and a girl," said Randall.

"We will be good parents, and we will never separate our kids from each other," I said as I looked at that handsome face and into those brown eyes.

"That's right, girlfriend," Randall said as he reached across the table for my hand and kissed it.

After our anniversary dinner, we went to his house, hung out for about an hour, and then I went home. That night after I got home and dressed for bed, I lay down to watch TV. All of a sudden, I felt something moving in my stomach. It felt funny, so I thought I had a stomachache. After all, we had dinner at McDonald's.

This movement went on for a few more days. It felt like something was pulling on my navel. It would happen for a few moments, and then it would stop. I wouldn't feel the movement again for a while. It was off and on, day in and day out.

A week had passed, and I finally figured out what was happening. Dare I say it? I was pregnant. It was time to tell Randall.

When I did tell him, we were over at one of our friend's house. I knew I had to tell him first, so I went without Teresa. I wanted to wait until I got his reaction before I told her.

"What's up, handsome boyfriend?"

"I'm good. How's my girlfriend?"

"Can we go into the kitchen and talk?" I asked as I grabbed his hand.

"Yes. What's up, Cindy?"

"I guess the best way to say this is to just come right out with it."

"What is wrong?" Randall asked.

"I'm pregnant." I just blurted it out.

He looked at me and said, "Cynthia, do not play around like that because I am not ready to be a father."

"Cynthia. Wow! You haven't called me that in a while." He never called me by my full name unless he was mad at me. "I'm not playing around. It's true, Randall. I'm pregnant."

"What are you going to do?" Randall asked with a look on his face that said, "I hope she's not going to keep this baby."

"I'm going to keep my baby."

"I do not know how to take care of a baby," said Randall.

After talking about it for an hour, he left. I had a feeling I wouldn't hear from him again. Another love lost, this time to pregnancy. I was okay with that because losing people I loved was becoming a part of my life. I still think about William and my grandma.

When I told Teresa, the first thing she asked was, "Are you sure you're pregnant?"

"Well, something has been moving around in my belly for a while now, and it is not gas."

"Well, let's go to the doctors to get confirmation to be sure," said Teresa. "Did you tell Randall?"

"Yes, and he said he's not ready to be a father. It's nothing I can do about that, but if I am, I am keeping my baby. Right now I'm just worried about what Barbara is going to say when I tell her."

"Yeah, that is going to be something," replied Teresa.

"I told you he was going to be my baby's daddy. Although getting pregnant before finishing school was not part of the plan. I did have a better picture of us being parents much later in the relationship. Hell, girl, we even talked about it. I thought I found my soul mate."

"We'll make an appointment for next week," said Teresa.

Teresa went with me, and before we left, the pregnancy was confirmed. I was four months along.

On the way home, Teresa asked, "When are you going to tell your mother?"

"Not today, that's for sure. I don't know, and I need to get used to this pregnancy myself," I told Teresa as I thought about the hell I would go through when I did tell dear Barbara.

For a couple of weeks, I walked around the house in sweat suits and big shirts. I spoke with Randall again, and his feelings were still the same as when I first told him I was pregnant. He still wasn't ready to be a daddy. At least he wasn't denying that he was the father. Should I be happy for small favors?

A few more weeks had passed, and I was starting to show. Avoiding Barbara was working until she came into my room while I was lying in my bed and asked, "Cynthia, are you pregnant?" The look in her eyes and tone of her voice brought about immediate fear. I wasn't sure if she really knew, and I wasn't at the admission stage.

"No." Then I thought, *I had better get up from this bed so I can be somewhat prepared for what is to come next.*

"Because if you are, I will tie your feet to some bricks and throw you in the Delaware River," Barbara commented as she walked out of the room.

There was no way in hell I was going to tell her anytime soon or alone for that matter. So after about a week, I went back to the doctors and told them they had to call my mother and tell her.

When she showed up and the doctor told her, she gave me a look that said, "You are in big trouble." On the way home, she asked, "Why couldn't you tell me this yourself?"

"I was scared of what you would do."

"We can't all stay in this house. There's not enough room, and who do you think is going to take care of that bastard child?"

I had no idea how to respond to that, so I decided that silence was my only answer. When we were inside the house, I followed her into the kitchen. A few more words about all my disappointments were said before Barbara grabbed a bag of flour from the counter, poured it over my head, and walked out of the room. All I could do was stand there and cry. After what seemed like a lifetime in a five-minute time span, I ran upstairs, took a shower, and ran over to Teresa's house to tell her what my mother had done.

Several months of hell with my mother, and then finally my son was born. It was the twenty-third of July. That night, I was more afraid of my mother's reactions to my going into labor than the delivery of my son. I didn't know if she would finally be a comforting mom or just matter-of-fact about the situation.

It all began around ten o'clock. My water broke while I was doing the dishes. When I told her my water had broken, she said, "Just go to your room and lay down. It's going to be a while. We will wait for Denise. She will be home soon." I was in so much pain, but I said nothing. I just cried and dealt with the pain in silence.

My sister arrived a half hour later. My mother and I sat in the back seat of the car, and every time she asked if I was okay, I just lied and said, "Yes." My first scream from having labor pains was finally released once I was in the delivery room because doing it in front of my mother wasn't going to happen.

After several more hours of labor, I gave birth to a seven-pound, eight-ounce baby boy who I named Kyle. Randall was there to see him the next day, but his feelings were still the same. He wasn't ready to be a father. He said, "I'm sorry" and left.

A few weeks later, after I got home from the hospital, my mother decided to hold Kyle for the first time. He must have sensed the evilness in her because he cried every time she touched him. Actually, he cried the entire time she held him in her arms. Soon her attitude toward him was no different from the one she had with me. I wanted to run away, but I had to think of Kyle. I dealt with it all the best way that I could; and, I did my best to stay away from my mother as often as I could.

The summer was over, and it was time to go back to school. Teresa's sister watched Kyle while I completed my last year of high school.

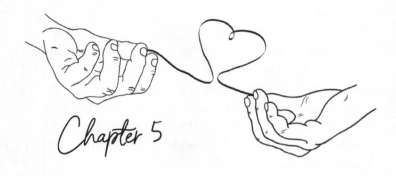

Chapter 5

The fall after Teresa and I graduated from high school, we went off to separate colleges, so we lost touch with each other for a while. She went to Lincoln University, and I went to Cheyney State. It was Kyle and I against my crazy family, with no Teresa to run to for a peaceful environment. My brothers were still at the house while Patricia and Denise were living at the dorm of their university, Temple. I commuted back and forth while Teresa's sister continued to watch Kyle.

I met a new friend on the first day of classes. Her name was Christine Allen. She was quiet, and you could tell she was a homebody. One thing we had in common was that she was also raised by her grandmother. But she did know her mother, and she was very nice. Her grandmother, whose name was Geneva, was raising Christine, and she was one of the sweetest women I had ever met. Soon her family became my family. I found love again in the way of a real family environment. They gave me a sense of belonging, and Kyle became very attached to Christine's grandmother. Grandma Geneva reminded me of my grandma through her kindness and generosity. She talked to me about being a good mother to Kyle. We talked about my feelings toward my mother and that before they destroy me, how I should learn to let them go. She became a very important part of my life. She was truly a blessing from God.

It was so good to find some type of love. It was out there in so many forms. With Teresa, it was friendship love that brought us as close as sisters. Now with Christine, it was family love because they made me feel like I was a member and not just someone Christine knew. I remember the tears that rolled down my face when she said, "Cynthia, our home is also your home." We were sitting on her bed, and she pulled me into her arms and wiped the tears from my face.

Christine also had a nephew who was Kyle's age, and they became best friends. Boy, did I spend a lot of time at Christine's house. Between Teresa and Christine's house, my son and I were doing okay.

Then the day came when I finally had a chance to introduce Teresa to Christine. Teresa had come home for her sister's birthday party, and I invited Christine so that she could meet Teresa. When Christine and I got to the party, Teresa spotted me right away. After the initial hugging and jumping up and down from being glad to see each other, I introduced Christine to Teresa. Christine stuck her hand out, but Teresa pulled her in for a hug. Then she said to Christine, "Anyone who is a friend of

Cynthia's is a friend of mine." Christine smiled, and we all walked outside to talk. We talked about school, the new man Teresa had met, and then we decided to go see our old friends, taking Christine with us.

When the evening ended, and Christine and I went back to her house, she told me she had fun. I knew there wouldn't be any jealousy between them because of who Christine was. Christine was a very unselfish person who only wanted everyone to be happy. Teresa just wanted me to have people in my life who loved me. Before we went to sleep, Christine told me that Teresa asked her to keep an eye on me and make sure that I laughed a lot.

From time to time, we would get together and have sleepovers. That is until Teresa met someone at Lincoln who lived in Pittsburgh. I saw her less and less until we lost contact again.

Things were going great until the day Kyle asked for his father.

"Mommy, where is my daddy?"

"He's away at college." That was the only answer I could think to give him at the time. Thank God for the short attention span kids had. He accepted my answer and ran off to grab a toy. Kyle was getting older, and I wanted him to know his dad. It had been two and a half years since I had spoken to him. I knew where he lived, so I thought I would go looking for him. Maybe we could find our way back to each other.

It was late in the evening, so I decided to wait until morning to start my search to bring my son and his father together.

After putting Kyle to bed, with the quiet time that was now with me, I lay in my bed, thinking about how to find someone to be with, whether it would be my son's father or someone else. Someone who would take my son and me away from this mad house I had to call home.

The ringing of the phone brought me out of my thoughts. I got up to answer it. "Hello."

"Is Cynthia there?" asked the man on the other end of the line.

"This is Cynthia. Who's this?"

"Randall. I see you do not recognize the sound of my voice. Anyway, I want to come by and talk to you, if I can?"

"When do you want to meet?" A smile was on my face as I started picturing his face.

"Can I come by tomorrow?" Randall asked.

"Sure. So does this mean that you are ready to be a daddy to Kyle now?" I asked.

"Yes. I see you did not name him after me. You told me our son would be named after his father. I guess my not being there for you changed that. We will talk tomorrow," he replied.

"Okay. Bye, Randall."

I remember hanging up and thinking, *How could he think I would name our son after him?* When he came to the hospital after our son was born, I told him then that if he wasn't going to be a dad to our son that his son would not carry his name. I told him he had ten days to decide on what he was going to do. He never called or came back.

This call from Randall gave me hope. At least that's what I thought. If nothing else, I could get Kyle out of this house, and he could have family love. I called Christine and told her that Randall was coming to see his son. It was late, so I told her I would call with the details in the morning.

I decided to wait until he showed up to tell my mother. I didn't want her to the ruin the visit, and if he didn't show up, I didn't want to hear the reasons she would give as to why he didn't come.

Randall showed up at the house around noon looking so damned good.

"Hey, Cynthia, how are you doing?" he asked as he leaned over to kiss me on the cheek. I wanted to pull him into my arms.

"I'm okay. Going to college and taking care of our son. What brings you here now, or shall I say what made you decide you were ready to be a father to your son?" There was a little sarcasm in my voice. I couldn't let him think I had forgiven him completely for deserting us. We were supposed to be in love. We were making life-long plans. To prove my point, I held in every smile that wanted to appear on my face. It was easy in that I just thought about the hell I went through with my mother whenever I felt a smile coming to the surface.

"I have been thinking, and I want to be a part of my son's life. I can't change what was done, but I can make it right now. I did call you a year ago, and your mother answered the phone. She told me you did not want to talk to me and not to ever call there again. I went away to college, and when I got back home, I thought I would try to call you again."

"My mother never told me you called."

"Well, here I am now. I'm not going back to college, and I'm living at home. Where is he? Can I see him?"

"Come on. He's in bed taking his nap." When we got in the room, he stood there and stared at him the same way he did when he saw him at the hospital the day he was born. Then he looked up at me and said, "I'm so sorry." Just as he did when I told him I was pregnant and when he first saw our son and still didn't want to be a father.

Then I just blurted out, "Do you have a girlfriend?"

He looked at me and said, "Yes."

Well, so much for thinking that I would come with the package. Destiny can't be avoided for it doesn't just happen; it arrives in its own time. We may have to detour a few times before finding the right love. I would get there. I just hoped it would be sooner rather than later. Even though this love was over, I was just happy he was ready to be a father.

Randall called several times every day to ask about his son. After reuniting with Randall for a month and during one of our many conversations, he said, "Cynthia, my mother wants to see her grandson. Can I come and get him on Saturday?"

"Sure, but I'm coming with you. You can't think that I would let you take him alone. Not right now."

"I know. It's fine. I didn't think you would let him go alone. I'll see you around ten tomorrow morning."

Seeing him still made me want him, but I knew it was over. I dressed Kyle in his best outfit. We were ready when his dad arrived. When we got there, his mother was very nice. I found out that Randall had just recently told his mother he was a father. She even pulled out a picture of

Randall when he was two years old to show how much our son looked like his father. Then his mother asked, "What are you doing with yourself, now that you are a mother?"

"I'm going to college. Teresa's sister watches my son."

"So, are you going to the community college?" Randall's mother asked.

"No, I'm going to Cheyney. I take the bus out from Sixty-Ninth Street."

"Well, I have a suggestion that can work for all of us. You can stay on campus, and my grandson can stay here. I feel that we owe you that much. What do you think?" She looked over at Randall, and he looked over at me.

"I'll be here with them," said Randall. "I have a part-time job working from eight in the morning to noon. After that, I will be with him. He will be fine."

"I don't know. I haven't been away from my son since he was born, but I'll think about it and let you know," was my response.

This offer was a gold mine. I could spend a year on campus and accomplish maybe three things in the process. One, I'll have another year of college under my belt; two, I could meet someone; and three, I would be out of my mother's house during the week. I intended to come home for Kyle every weekend. So after thinking about it for a week and having a few battles with the family, I said yes.

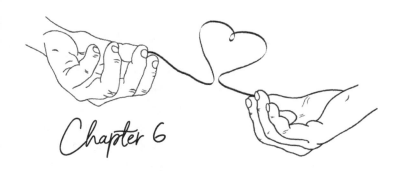

Chapter 6

My roommate's name was Rochelle Smith. Rochelle was from Chester and was looking for a way to get out of her neighborhood. She was also a very flirtatious girl who had decided that she would always be single and enjoy life to its fullest. She was entering her second year, and we took to each other right away. She was very sociable, so we always had people in our room. It was also pledge season for the social clubs that were on campus. There was this one called 307 Beta that interested me, so I decided to pledge. It was a male and female social organization. I tried to get Rochelle to pledge, but she had other plans. She was there for me whenever I needed her, even when she wanted to be free to hang out after her classes.

There were ten pledges on my line. It was called a line because of the formation. We stood in a line at all times when we were being pledged. The most the pledges did during the day was to carry a big brother's or sister's books to class if we ran into one of them on the way to class. Otherwise, the pledges always came together at dinner. We would march to the cafeteria and serve dinner to the big brothers and sisters before we could sit down to eat. After dinner, the females would go to one of the big sister's room. This was when we got together to learn about the social organization. When we weren't being taught about the organization, we were running around doing things based on the sisters' requests.

A few weeks into pledging, I met Nathan Brown. Nathan was in his last semester, majoring in accounting. We ran into each other while I was in his dorm collecting money to purchase books for the library. This was one of my many pledging assignments. Nathan was 5'8" tall with brown eyes. He was a slender man with a nice upper body, legs like tree trunks, and deep dimples. He was very handsome, and he didn't have a roommate—a big plus. When I wasn't at the sisters' beck and call, I would go over to his room where we would spend time studying.

Since he had pledged an organization, he would give me tips on how to be a good pledge. When the brothers and sisters came up from other colleges, they always wanted tuna fish sandwiches and soda. Nathan kept a supply for me.

It wasn't until after the pledging was over that we became intimate. He wanted to wait until then because during pledging, we couldn't really hang out. When we did, we went to the movies, for walks around campus, and to the mall. It was also a good thing I did meet Nathan because my roommate was always entertaining with the occasional overnight guest. We knew that this would end when the semester was over. Nathan was moving to Atlanta, and I couldn't go with him. This was the first time I wished that my son's father wasn't in the picture. I would have gone with Nathan. The job he had was paying a good salary, and he told me that I could complete my degree there. All I had to do was transfer my credits.

I asked Kyle if he wanted to move to our very own house, and all he could ask me was, "Is Daddy coming with us?" When I told him no, he said he wanted to stay with Daddy. I just couldn't take my son away from his father.

After Nathan's graduation, we went away for a few days before saying goodbye. It was an interesting year, but I still couldn't leave with a love on my arms.

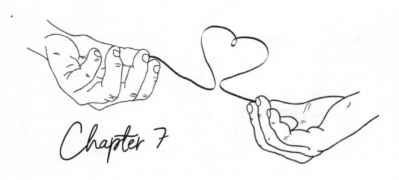

Chapter 7

I decided to take a year off from school and returned to being a full-time mother to Kyle. I continued to let his father's mother watch him during the week. It was what she wanted, and he was happy there. My mother also helped to make that decision by treating us the same as always. I didn't have money because I wasn't working, and she said she wasn't going to pay for a sitter. She wasn't happy about the decision I had made the previous year to let Kyle's father into his life.

Although Teresa was away at college, I still spent some time at her house. Her sister was there for those moments when things were hard between my mother and me. There was also a cousin living with them named Brenda Lowry. She reminded me of Rochelle. She was a little hard-core and very protective of her friends. She would tell you exactly what you needed to hear about things that bother you. No sugarcoating with her. She loved to party.

She and I became friends. When I wanted to go out to the clubs, and that, of course, wasn't Christine's scene, I would ask Brenda.

It was Valentine's Day, and I was feeling lonely when Brenda called and asked if I wanted to hit the club. *Why not?* I thought. *No one else was asking.* I didn't have to worry about Kyle because he was with his father. So I put on a red turtleneck cashmere sweater, a pair of black jeans, and my red pumps. Brenda met me out front at eight o'clock that evening, and we were on our way.

When we got there, Brenda went straight to the dance floor, and I went to the bar. I sat next to a man who I thought was good-looking. I ordered a glass of wine, and when the bartender came back, he offered to pay for my drink.

"Thank you," I said.

"You're welcome. What's your name?" he asked with a smile.

"Cynthia, and what's yours?"

"Daniel Hopkins."

We spent the next hour talking about this and that. I learned that he was five years older than I was and had his own place. So before Brenda and I left, I gave him my number. I knew at that moment I was doing it for the wrong reason, but I needed to get out of my mother's house. Daniel was Caucasian and would be my first interracial relationship. Love doesn't have a color, and right now, I needed someone. Besides, he was nice enough of a man for me to give a chance. I wasn't the first black woman he dated. He was Tom Cruise cute and had a similar build to Randall. He had his own place and a great job as a controller. No children or current ex-girlfriend. He had just come out of a five-year relationship, so to me, that was a sign of stability. However, I won't introduce him to my son until I'm sure he's okay.

On the way home, Brenda told me how many numbers she collected and how much fun she had. I told her about Daniel, and she said, "Go for it."

Daniel and I had been dating for four months when he decided it was time for us to live together. We were out to dinner, and the waitress had just left the table from taking our order for dessert when Daniel grabbed my hand and said, "Cindy, we have been seeing each other every day, and I find myself falling in love with you."

While listening to him, in my mind I was thinking he was going to ask me to marry him, and that was not what I wanted. Then I heard him say, "Move in with me because I have decided that I want to be with you every night and wake up with you every morning."

He was sweet, kind, and giving. We were having a lot of fun together, and the sex was great. He always asked about my son and bought him gifts. At this point, I hadn't introduced my son to any of the men I had been seeing. I didn't know where the relationships were going, so I felt it was the right thing to do.

Daniel was different. He was mature and responsible. So I responded with "I'm not sure I can do that right now, Daniel."

"Cindy, tell me why not? It's not like we don't spend a lot of time together," he reasoned.

"I have my son to consider when I decide to move out of my mother's house. Although he is spending the week at his father's house, I do get him every weekend and sometimes during the week. There are also times when I just go and spend the day with him at his father's house. Moving in with you makes it harder for me to get around. Plus, I don't even know if you are ready for a ready-made family."

"I know that with you comes your son. That is not a problem for me."

"I have to be honest, Daniel. I am not in love with you. I do care deeply for you."

"I know that. Why don't we just try it to see what happens. We can go get your things tomorrow."

"Yes. I will stay with you during the week, but I will go home on the weekends to be with Kyle. When I am sure about where we are going in our relationship, I will look at you meeting my son."

After living together for about two months, I decided it was time for him to meet Kyle. First, I had to tell Randall about Daniel. Although I knew about his girlfriend, I never told him about the men I dated. Since we would now be spending the weekends with Daniel, Randall had the right to know where his son would be staying. It was just a matter of respect, so when I told him, there wasn't an issue.

Anyway, we went to pick him up from his father's house. When I introduced Daniel to Kyle, Kyle reached out and took his hand like a little man. Then he asked Kyle, "What would you like to do today?"

"I want to go to the zoo," Kyle replied as he grabbed my hand and started walking toward the car.

"Well, let's see if it's okay with Mommy."

"Sure. It's early, and he does love the zoo. We can pick up a turkey sub, chips, and some drinks on the way."

Kyle took to Daniel, which made the weekend great. He played ball with him, and we took him to the movies. From that weekend on, I completely moved out of my mother's house, and we began living as a family. I had my son with me, and he was now visiting his father on the weekends. Although Randall was used to his son living with him, we didn't have a problem with the change. I was very grateful for what Daniel and Randall were doing for my son and me.

Kyle spent the rest of the summer going to amusement parks, on picnics, and to the movies. Between Daniel and Randall, my son was having a ball, and I was happy. Then one day while the three of us were having dinner at home, Daniel asked Kyle, "How would you like to move into a house?" The apartment we were living in was a one-bedroom and den.

Kyle asked, "Will I have a bigger room?"

"Yes. Now go to your room and play. I want to talk to Mommy," replied Daniel.

Daniel began to tell me about the house we were going to live in. It was his mother's house. She was moving to Atlanta to be near her sister.

We moved into the house two weeks later, just before the school year started. Kyle would be starting kindergarten.

A month later, Daniel bought me my first car. It was a burgundy four-door Mustang. It was on a Sunday when I got the car. We were sitting on the sofa watching a football game. At halftime, he got up to go get something to drink and came back with a card in his hand. "Here, honey."

"What's this for?" I asked.

"It's a token of my love for you. Open it."

"What is this?" A set of car keys fell out the envelope.

"Read the card, Cindy," he said with a smile on his face.

As I opened the card, I noticed his handwriting, so I read that part first. It said, "School will be starting for you soon. Yes, I want you to go back to college, and here is your means of transportation."

I looked up at him and smiled with tears in my eyes. I felt love for him at that moment. He wanted the best for my son and me. How could I not love him?

I couldn't wait to tell Christine, but she was away for the summer visiting her mother. I registered for classes to coincide with Kyle's schedule. He had afternoon kindergarten.

When Christine got back in late September, I told her all about my summer, and she told me about the man she met. His name was Marc, and she was in love.

Marc would come and visit Christine on the weekends. After about a month, she began to tell me how much she missed him when they were apart. She was my best friend, and I wanted her to be happy, so I asked Daniel if Marc could come and stay with us. We had four bedrooms, so he could stay in the spare room. I even mentioned how we would end up with a great built-in babysitter when she and Marc were together, especially because Christine didn't like going out that much.

He wasn't too hot on the idea at first, and I had a feeling it was because he didn't want me to be alone in the house with another man. I managed to talk him into it. When I told Christine he could come and stay at my house, she was very happy. She called Marc that night to let him know, and he was on the bus the next day. The four of us were one big happy family.

One afternoon when we were just sitting around, we decided to take the boys to the park. Christine had her nephew for the weekend. It was a nice fall day, and they could play basketball. I could see as time had passed how much love Christine had for Marc. So as we sat on a bench watching the boys play ball, I asked Christine, "What is it that you love about Marc?"

"Well, he makes me laugh, and he is an animal in bed," stated Christine. "So what is it about Daniel that you love?"

"He's good to me and my son. He knows I was trying to get away from my mother, so he asked me to move in with him. I told him at the time I didn't love him, and that didn't matter. Now I do, but I wish I was in love with him. I still have feelings for Kyle's daddy, so I can't give him my all."

"Does he know you still have feelings for Randall?"

"No! I can't tell him that. Although I think he knows."

"What makes you think he knows?" Christine asked. She momentarily turned and yelled to the boys, "Let's go get some ice cream!"

"When we go to pick Kyle up from his father's, he says I stare too hard at Randall and spend too much time inside his house."

"Sounds to me like he's jealous," stated Christine.

"Yes, he is. It's what I hate about him. We spend too much time arguing about someone who will never be in my life." This discussion ended when we both found ourselves calling to the boys to slow down.

When I got home, Daniel had dinner waiting for us. He had ordered Chinese food. While we were sitting at the table, he asked Kyle if he had fun at the park. I was always touched with the way he cared for Kyle. We finished dinner, and while I washed the dishes, they sat and watched TV.

For the next year, things were really going great. That is, until I ran into a man from college, who was in the same organization I had pledged, in the supermarket.

When he saw me, he gave me a hug, and before I could say anything, he kissed me on my lips. That just pissed Daniel off. He grabbed my arm and pulled me beside him. I introduced them, and Daniel walked away. After a few more words with him, I caught up with Daniel. Once we got in the car, he let me have it. The argument was so bad that I told him I was leaving him if he didn't get his jealousy under control. Things cooled off for a while when we got home, but later that night, the arguing started all over again.

It was the weekend, so Kyle was at his father's house. We were in the bedroom talking about the man at the market yet again. He said to me, "The only men you should be talking to are the ones your mother gave birth to."

I responded with, "Have you lost your mind? You are telling me whom I can talk to now and that I can't talk to a man unless it's one of my brothers or Kyle's dad. No, wait, you probably don't want me talking to Randall either."

"What reason do you need to be in a man's face anyway?" asked Daniel.

"Look, this conversation is a waste of time. I'm living with you, and I have no interest in anyone else. There will be men whom I know that I may run into, and you just need to accept that." Before I could say another word, he moved over to me and put me up against the wall.

Christine must have heard me telling him to get off me because she was knocking on the door, asking me if I was okay. Daniel yelled at her to mind her business. I yelled out to her, "No!"

She called for Marc, and he came up and pushed the door open. When Marc got him out the room, I grabbed some clothes and told Christine I was going to stay at my mother's house. I called Christine the next day to let her know I wasn't coming back.

Daniel tried for weeks to get me back. The thing was, I had promised myself if any man ever put his hands on me, I would leave and never come back. His jealousy was a sure sign that it would happen again. Why was it so hard for me to find the relationship that I desired? They all started out so great, and then after about a year or so, for one reason or another, they failed.

Relationship number 4 had gotten away from me. My William, I lost him when my grandma took me from him. My Randall, I lost him when I told him I was pregnant. My Nathan, I lost him because I didn't want to move my son away from his father. Now, my Daniel, I lost him to the green-eyed monster.

I'm still not giving up on love. I have plenty of love to give, and someone was waiting for it. We just had to meet. Only God knows when and where that meeting will take place. For now, it was back to my mother's house for my son and me. The only good thing about this move was that she was no longer living there. She and her husband moved to Germantown, but she decided to keep the family home. Said she wanted her kids to always have a place to come back to when things got rough. Lucky me. Only my three brothers and their girlfriends were living there now.

I took the third floor for my son and me. Christine eventually moved back home, and Marc went to stay with a sister who lived nearby.

Chapter 8

A few months had passed, and that lonely feeling was back again. I was attending my classes, and my son was going to an elementary school near his father. I would pick him up from his father on my way in from class, play with him for a while, get him ready for bed, study, and then fall asleep watching TV.

I wanted a companion, so it was time to go man hunting again. Time to give love another try.

One day on campus, I saw Rochelle. She was registering to take classes during the fall semester. We hadn't seen each other since we were roommates, so after talking for a while, we exchanged numbers, and I went to class. I called her and asked if she wanted to go out on Friday. We decided we would meet up at her house.

We went to a bar in Chester. We were sitting at the bar talking about her adventures since we last met. When she went to order another drink, I turned around on my stool to see who was in the bar. I noticed a man who was leaning against the wall in motorcycle gear. We held eye contact long enough for us to smile at each other. I turned back around and asked Rochelle, "Do you know that man in the biker's gear standing against the wall?"

She looked to see who I was referring to and said, "Yeah, his name is Robert Thomas. You want me to introduce you?"

"Nope, I can do that myself. I've never had a problem going up to a man and introducing myself."

I walked over to him and said, "I've never ridden on a motorcycle before. Would you take me for a ride?" Hey, men usually walk up to a woman with some lame line like "Don't I know you?" So why couldn't I?

"And your name would be?" he asked.

"Cynthia. And yours?"

"Robert. So you're willing to go for a ride with a man you don't know?"

"Well, my girlfriend knows you." I pointed over to Rochelle.

"Are you pointing to Rochelle?" When he looked over at her, she waved to him.

"Yes. So what about taking me for a ride?" I asked.

"Okay. Let's go."

I told Rochelle we would be back in an hour.

We hit it off and started hanging out quite a bit. I saw him on Tuesdays and every other weekend. I told him I had a son, and he wanted to meet him, but I told him it wasn't time yet. I had to be sure there would be a relationship before that happened. We had only been seeing each other for two weeks when we went on our first real date. It was at a club in Media. This was the get-to-know-you date.

"So where do you live, Robert? I've been seeing you for a couple of weeks, and you haven't invited me to your place."

"I live at home with my mother."

I wouldn't be moving in with him anytime soon.

"What kind of work do you do?"

"I work at an auto parts store. I've been working there for ten years."

A little more of his family history, and we moved on to me.

"So what do you do, Miss Cynthia?"

"I'm going to college. I'm in my final year."

"That's nice. So what are you majoring in?"

"I'm majoring in accounting."

"So when am I going to meet this son you keep talking about?"

"Like I told you before, I think we should get to know each other a little more before that happens."

"That's fair enough. Is his father still around?"

"Yes. They spend a lot of time together."

"Would you like to dance?" he asked.

"Sure."

The evening went fairly well.

Three months had passed, and I finally introduced him to my son. We took him to the movies and then out to dinner. We all had a nice time.

A few more outings, and then bang, our first bit of drama. Rochelle and I had gone to a party that he was having with some friends at a club in Chester. There were two areas to this club. As you entered the club, you were in the bar area, and in the back was the dancing area. Rochelle and I stayed up front. Robert worked both ends of the club showing me some attention throughout the night to make sure I wasn't feeling neglected.

When we were leaving and I was getting ready to get on his bike, an orange Volkswagen came speeding through the parking lot. It stopped in the driveway where no one could get in or out. Some woman was yelling something out to Robert. I asked him what she was saying, but before he could respond, Rochelle was pulling me away from him.

"Let's go, Cynthia," she said.

"No. I'm riding with Robert. You take the car like we discussed earlier."

"No, you're not. We're getting in the car."

"Leave her alone," said Robert. "She's riding with me. We're going to the clubhouse. You can meet us there."

"She's not riding with you, Robert," replied Rochelle.

Rochelle pulled me away, and she held on to me until we got to the car. On our way to the clubhouse, she asked, "Cynthia, what do you think is going on here, and why would you think about getting on that bike when that girl threatened to run your man over?"

"I guess Robert pissed that girl off. He has a gift for doing that. I couldn't hear what she was yelling, but I got that she was mad."

"So you didn't hear what she was saying?"

"No, I didn't."

"Then hear what I am saying to your ass. She was threatening to run you and Robert over if he let you ride on his bike. Look, Cynthia, when you called and told me about the party, I didn't even know that you were still see-ing Robert. I hadn't spoken to you since that night at the bar. Robert has a girlfriend, and that was her."

"He told me he didn't have a girlfriend. Wait until we get to the clubhouse!"

Rochelle wanted me to go home, but that was not an option.

When we arrived at the clubhouse, Robert and the girl were at her car talking. I started walking toward them when Rochelle pulled me back and said, "Come on, Cindy, let's go inside the clubhouse. Down, girlfriend, take it easy."

When he came in, he walked over to where I was sitting with a smile on his face and asked, "Is everything okay?"

"So who was she?" I asked.

"She was an old girlfriend. We broke up six months ago, and this was the first time she saw me out with another woman. She's been trying to get back with me, but it is over. I reminded her of that again tonight."

"Well, you can just tell her you are free. This rela-tionship is over." I grabbed Rochelle and told her I was ready to leave.

I stopped seeing Robert that night. I didn't have time for girlfriend drama. On the way home from the club, I vowed to give up men for a while. Here I was again. I just needed to stick with studying and raising my son.

Chapter 9

I ran into Robert six months later while at a club with Rochelle. We talked for a while about what was going on with our lives since we last met. Then I asked, "Are you still seeing your drama queen girlfriend?"

He grabbed my hand and said, "Look, I'm still a single man, and I want to get to know you. Can I take you to the movies?"

"I don't know. I'm not the one for girlfriend drama."

"There won't be any drama," replied Robert.

"Okay. I'll go. Give me a call, and we'll make plans for a night soon." I said goodbye and went back to where Rochelle was sitting.

Robert and I went to the movies a week later. After the movies, we went back to his mother's house where he was still living. His bedroom was up on the third floor. We had sex, which, for the most part, was good. I kept thinking someone was going to come upstairs, so my entire focus wasn't on the act. I was ready to leave when we were done, but he asked me to stay. I made sure I was out of there before anybody woke up.

A month later, I realized I was carrying his child. Oops. Just call me Miss Fertile. This was not what I wanted. I was getting ready to graduate from college, find a job, and now I was with child. All I thought about was *Damn, a second child, a second daddy, and I'm not in a real relationship with either of them. What am I going to do now?*

I was not going to be living in my mother's house with a second child. Even though she wasn't living at the house, she was still in control of what was going on there. She still paid the bills, bought the food, and she came by the house every day. The constant statements about how I had ruined my life and how no man was going to want a woman with a baby was more than I could take.

I knew I had to decide on whether or not I wanted to keep this child. If I did, would Robert be a good father? I guess the first question would be, does he want to be a father? I'd worry about that later. No matter what, it was time for me to start looking for my own place.

I thought about asking Rochelle if she wanted to get a place together, but then I remembered she had a very heavy social life. It wouldn't work out because the environment wouldn't be good for Kyle. So the search for my own apartment was on.

What I didn't know was that while I was looking for a place to live, my dear old mother had other plans for my son's new place of residence. It was on a Saturday, and I had been out looking for an apartment all morning.

When Kyle and I got home, I went straight to my room to lay him down for a nap.

My mother was at the house in the kitchen cooking. She came into the room and said, "Cynthia, I'm putting Kyle in Girard College. It's a school for boys without fathers."

"He has a father that he sees all the time, so he doesn't need to go there."

"Well, he can't afford to take care of the both of you," replied my mother.

"He doesn't need to take care of me, just his son. I don't want him to go, and you can't take him away from me. He can go and live with his father."

"We're leaving in the morning. Pack his things tonight."

"You are not taking my son away from me!"

I called Randall to let him know what was going on. He said he would come and get him. When he got there, my mother called the police. She showed them some papers that wouldn't allow Randall to take Kyle. Then I said to her, "Well, Kyle and I are leaving."

"No, you will be leaving without Kyle. I have partial guardianship of your son until you are twenty-one."

What the hell had she done? How did she manage to get that kind of control? That morning she took Kyle from me, and off they went. I cried off and on that entire day. My son did not belong in that school. He wasn't an unwanted child. His father may not have played a major role at the time, but I sure as hell wanted to be his mother in every sense of the word. She was not going to separate me from my son as she had separated herself from me. I had to get an apartment. I would be twenty-one soon, and she would be out of our lives for good.

In the meantime, I left home and went to live with Rochelle. I went to classes, and Randall and I visited with our son at the boarding school every weekend.

Robert and I continued dating, but I hadn't told him or anyone else about the baby yet. After my graduation, which was in December, I decided to move to Delaware. Delaware would be a nice medium for the fathers of my babies. Yes, I decided to keep the baby.

I reached out to Daniel and told him what my mother had done. He told me I could come back to his place, but I told him I wanted my own. He offered to give me whatever I needed to move in, which was the first month's rent and security deposit. A week before moving in, I made a call to let my son's father know. When I told him I was moving to Delaware, he yelled, "You're moving that far from our son?"

"No. First, it's only fifteen minutes from where I am now, and I'm doing this for my son and me. The schools are very good in Delaware. I'm away from my mother, and we will not be that far away from you. The only way for me to get him out of that school is to have my own place."

Once he understood everything, he said, "Alright, Cynthia. I'll give you half the rent."

I started to ask him where he was getting the money from, but it really wasn't my business. "Thanks. I'll be getting him out in June. You can start giving me the money then."

I moved into my apartment in January, and I started my job a few weeks later. I would be okay paying my rent alone for a while.

I had settled in for two weeks before inviting Robert. I prepared a nice dinner, and over dessert, I dropped the bomb. "Robert, I'm pregnant."

"What?"

"We are going to have a baby in a few months."

He got up, came over to me, and gave me a hug. He surprised me. He was excited, and we sat and talked about what our son was going to be like. At least Robert didn't reject me by saying he didn't want a child. He talked about how we needed to get an apartment. What impressed me the most was when he said, "We can start out with two bedrooms and get a third when our son is older. Kyle will have to share his room for a while. We will have it ready before school is out, and we bring him home."

Robert moved in a few days later. We had a baby boy, Robert Jr., and married shortly after his birth. Had I found my soul mate? The one true love I desired?

Chapter 10

Robert and I had been together for eleven years dealing with our difficulties, which were the usual issues couples go through. I loved him, but I never fell in love with him. Something was holding me back, and I didn't figure out what it was until he lost his job of fifteen years. It turned out to be his drinking. The drinking gradually increased as he became depressed from not working, and nothing I said to comfort him helped. We began a downward slope to the failure of our marriage. As the arguments grew—and they were ugly—the love I had for him began to fade.

He was out of work for two years before he got something down on the city docks. He started out as a part-time worker, but spent the whole day there. When he wasn't working, he sat around with the other men who also weren't working, playing cards and drinking. By the time he got home, he was drunk. We would get into arguments that became very abusive on a mental level, but there was that one argument that turned physical.

Christine had come down earlier on the train with her nephew to spend the day with me and the boys. I was working a night job in Philly, so on the way to work, I would drop the boys off at my mother-in-law's and Christine at home. Robert decided he wanted me to drop him off at a bar in Chester, but I told him no. He left the house, so I thought he had gone. However, when we got to the car, he was already sitting in the front seat. I said, "I'm not taking you to the bar."

"Then drop me off at Mom's house with the boys."

"Okay, fine."

He looked at me and called me a bitch and smacked me in the mouth. Now, I had my boys and my girlfriend in the car. My pride was at stake, so I reached over and smacked him back. After a few unmentionable words, the ones that had the most effect from him were, "When you stop this car, I'm going to kick your ass."

Now I knew I wouldn't win that fight, and I wasn't going to get my girl involved. So I put my thinking cap on and decided to take him to the police station. I started the car up, holding back the tears, and started driving, making a left out the parking lot instead of a right.

"Where the hell are you going?" he asked.

"I'm taking you somewhere so you can kick my ass."

"What the f—— are you talking about?"

"You will see soon enough."

When I pulled into the police station, I looked over at him and smiled. I got out the car, went over to his side, opened the door, and said, "I stopped the car. Come on and kick my ass."

He wouldn't get out the car, so I went into the station with tears in my eyes and told the officer that my husband was threatening to beat me up. I told the officer how he had popped me in my lip and that my kids were in the car and afraid.

The officer got him out my car, and I left him at the station. Christine waited until I dropped the boys off before she said anything.

"I'm glad you did what you did. You do know that I had your back?"

"Yeah, I know, but I wasn't going to put you in that position."

We changed the subject and talked about how much fun the boys had until I dropped her off at home. When I got home from work, he was at the house. With fear in my heart, I said, "Robert, I'm sick of all this arguing. It's not good for us or for the boys to hear, and I can't believe you hit me. You have got to go!"

"I'm not going anywhere."

"Please don't make this any harder than it already is."

"If I leave, I will not be back. You can't afford this place on a fucking part-time job. Where you gonna get the money from, your mom? She doesn't want anything to do with you."

"Oh yes, I can. I don't need you or my mother. I just want you gone."

He didn't know I was getting money from Randall, and there was no need to tell him now. After we said a few more nasty words to each other, he left.

Christine called that morning to see if I was okay. She was on her way to work, so I only had time to tell her that I was fine, and Robert was gone.

"Good, he doesn't deserve you. I'll call you on my lunch break," she commented before hanging up.

Later in the afternoon, I got a call from Rochelle and told her what had happened. Rochelle was never a fan of Robert.

"Girl, I'm glad you put him out. You will be okay. I'll help you as much as I can."

"Yeah, I know. He's not that bad when he's not drinking. I just can't continue to let the boys hear him talk to me the way he does when he's drunk."

"Come on, Cynthia, don't start making excuses for him. Anyway, let's talk about something more pleasant."

"Okay. So what's going on with you?" I asked as I tried to push last night out of my mind.

"Well, I'm planning a dinner party on Friday, and I want you to come."

"I don't know if I'll be able to get a sitter for the boys."

"You better. How about asking your mother-in-law?"

"I'll see. Their father will be there, so he'll get a chance to see them. I'll be there. You want me to bring anything?"

"Nope, I'm good with food. All is under control."

Since everyone was in Chester, I waited until it was time for the party to drop off the boys. Rochelle lived a few blocks up from my mother-in-law's house. That evening I met her uncle Cole Dawson. He was handsome, stood about six feet tall, and he was a serviceman. You couldn't miss that, being he was in an army uniform.

After spotting him, I went over to Rochelle and asked, "Who's the man in the army uniform?"

"He's my uncle Cole. He's home on leave for a couple of months."

I decided to be bold, so I walked over and introduced myself to him. Sure, I was stilled married, but the love was fading, and I wanted just a little happiness in my life, even if it was only for one night.

"Hi. My name is Cynthia, and I was told you are Uncle Cole. Your niece and I attended college together."

"She mentioned you to me earlier today. She said she had a friend named Cynthia that she wanted me to meet."

We both looked over at Rochelle and pointed our fingers at her. She smiled and continued chatting with the person in front of her.

Cole and I spent most of the evening talking. Before I left, he invited me out.

For the next two months, we spent every day together. We saw movies, went out to dinner, and we would sit and talk for hours. When it was time for him to leave, he wanted me to go with him, but I couldn't. I remembered the day he left. I was happy, and then it became very sad.

We had lunch in the park that afternoon when he said, "Cutie [that's what he liked calling me], I love you, and I want you and the boys to come live with me."

"But you haven't even met my boys," I replied. I knew this wasn't going to be a lifetime relationship, so there was no reason for him to meet them.

"I don't have to. They are a part of you, and therefore, they will be a part of us." Wow! He blew my mind with that statement.

"You want me to take them away from their father?"

"He's an asshole and don't deserve you."

"I can't do that, Cole. You move around too often from being in the service, and that is not a stable life for my boys. They need a foundation and to be near their fathers. As I told you, my oldest son's father is in Philadelphia, and he plays a part in his son's life."

I really wanted to go with this man, but I couldn't.

He said, "I don't want to spend what time we have left debating about what's good for us. You have to leave in an hour for home, and I'm leaving tonight. I will give you the rest of the day to think about it. If I don't hear from you before I leave for the airport, I'll have my answer."

When we went back to his place, we made love for the first time (protection used) before departing for the day. I knew I wouldn't see him again and that I was probably letting a good man get away.

Three months later, after a few counseling sessions, I let my husband return home.

Chapter 11

One day while shopping at the supermarket, I ran into Teresa. I was going up aisle 5, and she was coming down aisle 5. We walked right past each other, but you could see the look of acknowledgment on our faces. Within seconds, we turned to each other and started screaming. The few customers who were also in aisle 5 were looking at us, trying to figure out what was going on.

Teresa and I were hugging and jumping up and down as if we were on a trampoline. "What are you doing in Delaware?" I asked, still holding onto to her. I had my best friend back, and I didn't want to let go.

"We moved here a year ago for the schools," replied Teresa.

"So you're here for the schools?" I repeated.

"Yes, my husband and I wanted to raise our girls here," said Teresa.

"That's the reason I moved here. I'm married, and I have another son. I have two boys now. How many girls do you have?"

"Two. Megan is three, and Tasha Cynthia Jones is five. I can't wait to see your boys. I wonder if Kyle will remember me?" she asked.

"Tasha Cynthia? Ah, you gave her my name. Kyle was only one year old when you left. He's seventeen now, so I don't know. My other son's name is Robert. He's now ten."

We talked for about another ten minutes before we exchanged phone numbers and agreed to get together for dinner the following day. Reconnecting with Teresa was a gift from God, literally.

We had such a good time, so it wasn't hard for me to convince Teresa to spend the night. Teresa's husband was away on a business trip, so she agreed. Once we put the children to bed, we spent hours talking about our lives and love. When I told her about my marriage, she said, "Don't you dare give up on love. Plus, you and the boys can come and stay with me."

"I'll be okay. Giving up on love was never an option. I know my soul mate is out there looking for me, but it isn't time for us to connect."

"What are you saying?"

"My heart isn't at peace, so it can't find love."

"What's the problem?"

"I am still angry about my mother deserting me, and now there's the bitterness toward my husband. God won't send my soul mate until I'm deserving of him. I'm not saying God's punishing me because He isn't. I'm hurting myself, in turn, being the one blocking my blessing from him."

"I didn't know you were still mad at your mother. Let it go, Cindy, and the sooner you leave this bad marriage, the better."

We finally went to sleep around two in the morning. We were up by ten, fixed breakfast for the kids, and shortly thereafter, Teresa went home. It was the best day I had in a long time.

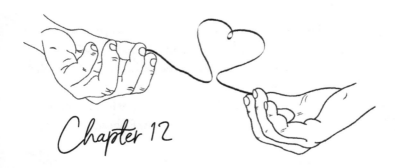

Chapter 12

My motivation for now was my children. I had to make sure they stayed with me no matter what obstacles came our way, even to the point of enduring a bad marriage. A marriage I tried to make work even when we were at our worst. No matter how much I tried, things just wouldn't turn around for us.

It was our nineteenth anniversary, so he asked me to get a sitter and plan a trip to a ski resort in Pennsylvania called Strickland. When it was time to leave, we dropped the boys off at Teresa's and got on the road.

The room we stayed in was nice. There was a red heart-shaped Jacuzzi in the bedroom, the bed was round, and there were mirrors on the ceiling. The first few hours were nice. When we walked into the room, he commented on how nice it was, and then he said, "I promise you this will be a nice weekend for the both of us."

"I'm going to hold you to those words. We can unpack later. I'm going to run a bubble bath, so why don't you grab the sparkling cider and the glasses from the small luggage bag and join me."

"I don't want any cider! Where the hell is the beer?"

"There won't be any beer tonight, Robert. Can't you give me this one weekend?"

"Can't I have at least one beer?" I could see he was getting mad, but I had to stand my ground on this issue.

"No. Either you give me this weekend, or we can just put the luggage back into the car and go home now."

"Okay. We'll do it your way for now." He put a mixed CD in the CD player and joined me in the Jacuzzi.

After few hours of passion, we then got dressed and went out to dinner. The waiter came over and asked, "What can I get you to drink?"

I ordered a soda, and Robert ordered a beer. I was getting ready to say something, but before I could, he looked at me and said, "I'm having a beer."

I realized my saying anything else would be in vain, and I wasn't going to argue with him in public. I simply got up and returned to the room. By the time he got there, he was drunk.

That morning I packed up our things and checked us out. On the way home, I said to him, "I am done trying to make this marriage work."

He looked at me and said, "So I got drunk this weekend. We were away, and I just wanted to enjoy myself."

"Why can't you enjoy yourself without getting drunk? It wouldn't be so bad if you knew when to stop, but you just keep on drinking until there's no more to drink or you run out of money. Then I have to deal with your drunken behavior."

"Are you calling me an alcoholic?"

"Yes, Robert, I am, but I have been calling you that for a while now. You act like it's the first time I called you that."

"Well, I'm not an alcoholic."

"Well, think what you want. I'm glad you enjoyed yourself because once we left the room for dinner, the rest of the night wasn't enjoyable for me. Your coming back to the room drunk certainly got in the way of that."

Once that conversation was over, we rode the rest of the way home in silence. I called Teresa when we got back in town. She told me to just leave the boys and pick them up tomorrow, as planned.

When I got to Teresa's the next day to pick up the boys, the kids were playing a game, and so we sat and talked for a while. I told her about how the night started out fine, and if we hadn't gone out to dinner, we may have survived an entire night of fun. "Damn me for not taking food with us," I commented.

Teresa said, "Girl, there will be a time when you find a good man, a man who will make you very happy. You need to leave this bad marriage."

"I know I shouldn't have stayed with Robert. I just wanted to be with the father of one of my boys, so I settled."

"I understand that's how you feel, but this is making you miserable. So what are you going to do about it now?"

"I'm going to see this through, at least until Robbie [Robert's nickname] finishes high school. I can only hope that things will change between us. I'm going to commit to my marriage vows for another year. At least make sure I have done everything I can to save my marriage. So that when I leave, I am free to search for my true love with no regrets."

"I'm here for you, Cynthia."

"I will end up with my true love, Teresa. My true love is doing his thing right now, so that when we come together, and after dealing with our own obstacles, we will spend the rest of our lives together in bliss."

We hugged, got the boys together, and I went home to cook dinner. I believed what I said to Teresa. I just needed to be free of my past so that I could love him with a pure and honest heart.

Later that night, I got on the computer and wrote a poem about my soul mate. It was called "Oh Love":

Oh love, you are living somewhere far or close,
because the two of us are looking for each other.
Oh love, I hope you are thinking of
me as I am thinking of you
Oh love, when we meet, I want to
accept you as a gift from
God and give myself to you unconditionally.
Oh love, you will know my heart and soul.
Oh love, you will fulfill all my dreams and all desires.
Oh love, please forgive me my faults.
I will be a little afraid because I will
have a damaged heart.
Oh love, I will pray for you tonight
with a promise from this
night that my heart will be faithful to you.

It is so easy to feel the love you desire. To envision what you would do when love comes your way. True love can be hard to find when there are motives. When motivation is not always pure, it clouds your judgment. Then there's the point when you do find it, you are so messed up from previous relationships that you end up pushing it away. "I ask you, God, to please help me to see it, and if I mess up at first, please guide me back to it."

A few months had passed, and things just weren't getting any better. The drinking got worse, and so did the arguing. We began talking to each other as though we were total strangers. It got to a point where I left my bedroom and began sleeping on the sofa. I didn't want the boys to know, so I made sure I was always up before them. I tried to shelter them from as much as I could of our problems.

One morning while taking Robert to work, he had the nerve to say something about me sleeping on the sofa. "You need to stop staying up so late watching TV. Maybe then you wouldn't be falling asleep on the sofa."

"I'm not falling asleep on the sofa because I'm up watching TV. I just don't want to sleep with you anymore."

"You think that is going to solve our problems?"

"There's no longer a problem to solve because the marriage is over. I'm tired of arguing with you. I'm tired of asking you to get help with your drinking. I'm tired of being embarrassed when we are out."

"I don't have a drinking problem." That was his last comment before getting out of the car.

I wanted to run him down, but I knew I couldn't. I went back home and got ready for work. I was still contemplating on when I could leave and if I was doing the boys any good by staying with this man.

I knew I couldn't raise two boys on my own, so I stayed. A couple of more years had passed, and things remained the same. There was no improvement at all. Thursday through Saturday was his weekend. He would go to work, come home drunk, drink some more, and find some reason to start an argument. I kept the boys away from home as much as I could. When they stayed at their friends, I stayed with Teresa, Christine, and sometimes with Rochelle.

I started thinking about the decision I made about being with Cole. Should I have gone with him? Even though the man I married was an asshole, he was a good provider, and the boys wanted for nothing. My oldest son's father was also in his life. He would visit him every other weekend. Therefore, I still convinced myself that no matter how much I thought about it, it was the right decision. Plus, Cole wanted kids, and two daddies were my limit.

In the evenings when the boys didn't require my attention, I would spend time on the computer. I would write poems and fantasies about what real love and true passion would probably feel like.

There were even times when I would babysit for my friends whom I worked with so that they could have date night as they tried to keep their marriage and love intact. To do what they could to bring out the best in each other. They would tell me how they didn't want to make their children their whole world and end up losing each other in the process. That keeping the family together and their relationship was not an easy task. They thought my life was good because I never gave them a reason to think anything was wrong at my home.

Their drive to make things work gave me hope. I built my hopes around their relationships. I knew I had a lot of love to give. So what good was having love and not being able to share it with someone worthy of giving it to? *My love will come.*

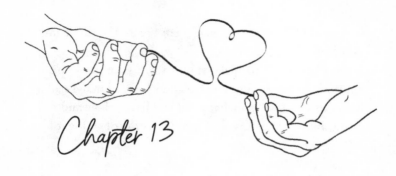

Chapter 13

Now that my husband and I were living as roommates, I was doing okay. Arguments did somewhat slow down because I was ignoring him. I finally learned that if I didn't argue back, the confrontation ended a lot sooner.

I had my best friend, Teresa, back in my life again. We agreed that whenever things were too much for me, I would give her a call, and we would talk and cry together. Things would be as they were in the past, when we were younger.

Teresa and I were growing close again and getting to know each other's closest friends. So we decided to form a girls' only night-out club. Once a month, we all got together and had what we called "how to love your man" night. The girls had relationships they wanted to save, and I wanted to find one. So it was not about man bashing.

There were five of us: Teresa, Marsha, Jackie, Rochelle, and me. Teresa was an at-home bookkeeper, married, with two girls, of course. Marsha was a receptionist at a doctor's office, living with her beloved (no children). Jackie was a housewife with one son, but she and her husband were also having problems. I was the accountant in the marriage from hell. Then there was Rochelle. She was a schoolteacher and didn't want a steady man. She just wanted to enjoy life and have as much fun as she could as a single woman until she couldn't party anymore. Rochelle was seldom there for our monthly hangouts.

Our girls' night out started with us sitting around talking about how most men just didn't get love the way we understood it. Even though Teresa and Marsha had good men, they talked about the ones they dated who weren't good and how glad they were for not giving up on love.

During one of our gatherings, Marsha said, "Ladies, why don't we start doing things to excite our men."

"Like what?" Teresa asked.

"Well, when was the last time any of us had a romantic dinner at home?" asked Marsha.

"I just had one last night," replied Rochelle. "That's how it goes when you are just dating. Speaking of which, ladies, it's been real, but I have to go. I've got a hot date again tonight and just enough time to get home and get sexy."

"That's our Rochelle," I said as she kissed me on the cheek before she left.

"Four years ago, my last daughter brought things to an end," replied Teresa as she shook her head. "Lord have mercy. Those were the good old days." Teresa grabbed her glass and finished the red wine left in her glass (about two fingers) before putting it down.

"Two years for me," commented Marsha. "Our work schedules get in the way, and the weekends are spent visiting our families. We need more wine." Marsha got up to go and get another bottle of wine from Teresa's wine bar.

"No romantic dinners for me," said Jackie. "I've had my son since the day we met, so we never found the time. Sure, we would go out to dinner, but nothing that would fall in the romantic passionate category. Now that I think about it, no wonder we're having problems! We're just too damn boring." She shook her head and then pulled her hair back, as if she was going to put it in a ponytail.

"What about you, Cindy?" asked Marsha.

"Well, I tried to plan a nice romantic trip to the Poconos. It started out great, but ended early because he got drunk. I'll try it because I am a little horny. Robert was asking for sex, I just wouldn't give him any."

"There's nothing wrong with having sex. He is still your husband. Okay, girls. Plan your meals and set things up," said Marsha.

We lifted up our glasses and made a toast to a successful evening of romance.

The following month, when we got together again, everyone was eager to talk about their dinner. So we had to come up with a system for who would go first. We agreed that from now on, stories would be told in first-name order, but to be fair, we would rotate each month.

They all served their meals in sexy lingerie except Marsha, who wanted to go au naturel under her apron. Everyone who tried had a good time. I wanted to try dinner with Robert, but by the time it was a good night for me to do it, he came home from work drunk. My plan was to cook in a maid's outfit while he was home. The boys were going to their grandmas, so I dropped them off and went shopping. I thought, *What the hell, I could use a night of passion and take another stab at my marriage.* It had been a while since I tried. I even called him at work and told him I had a surprise for him. He said he would be home right after work. Once again, he ruined things. He came home drunk. I found out that he only worked the morning shift, and they sat around playing cards and drinking (who knows what else they did). The outfit went back in the box that night and back to the store the next morning.

Anyway, from then on, when we got together, we talked about things to do to make the relationships better. Fantasies night, notes in briefcases, and phone calls in the middle of the workday. Marsha even suggested that we take the men out once a month for dinner and that we pay for it. She said, "Think of how it would make them feel if we paid for a meal. It makes us feel good, right?" The ladies agreed. I just took it all in so that I would be able to use these suggestions when I found my love.

A few more meetings, and they were talking about how their relationships and sex lives were improving. They insisted that we would have these nights until the end of time.

Chapter 14

My Kyle had graduated and gone off to college. Now it was just the three of us. I was no longer sleeping on the sofa because I moved into Kyle's room. My husband and I would only share the same bed on those rare occasions when I needed some sexual release. Even that eventually ended. I diverted my passion to the little things that brought me pleasure, such as writing poems and fantasies. Things moved on as usual as I waited for my youngest son to graduate from high school so that I could move out.

My mornings consisted of sitting out on the porch listening to the birds while I had my first cup of coffee for the day. Speaking of diverting passion, with the right frame of mind and imagination, I could say that the steam from a hot cup of coffee gave me a slight sense of passion. I would breathe it in and smile as I thought about making love (breathing in the scent of my love). It was the pure pleasure with the connection of two bodies feeling the heat of passion, which could be felt from the sexual release of lovemaking. When I went back into the house, I would be singing some melody that was a reflection of what I was feeling at that moment. I was ready for the day and any obstacles that would come my way.

After work, I made sure Robbie got his homework done, had dinner, and got to his evening activities. When he went out to be with his friend, all he had to do was be in by his curfew, which was set for eleven o'clock, although that wasn't always possible. The stories he would come up with for getting in late were good ones. There was one night when he came in rapping to the lyrics of a song by the artist 50 Cent. I stopped him and asked, "Why are you just getting in? You are a half hour late."

"No, I'm not, Mom," Robbie replied.

"Yes, you are."

Then he just walked back out the door.

I thought the boy had lost his mind until he came back in, saying, "The clock in the car said eleven o'clock."

Okay, as if I didn't know that trick. He had reset that clock with his story already planned.

I just shook my head and said, "Go to your room."

Anyway, once all was in order and it was downtime for me, I was back on my computer for hours. The computer was my friend.

The more I wanted love and passion, the more I realized that it was time for me to move on. My son would be graduating soon, and I could get out of this marriage.

I no longer had a reason for staying. I gave all that I could give based on the relationship, and no woman should allow herself to endure emotional or physical abuse from anyone, especially from someone who claims to love you.

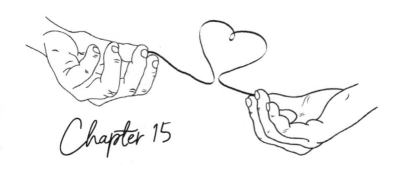

Chapter 15

Sunday, my son's graduation day, was the final nail in the coffin. By the time we left for the ceremony around eleven that morning, Robert was already intoxicated. There was no way I was going to allow him to embarrass us, so I stayed so close to him at the ceremony that you would have thought we were in love. He moved, I moved. When the ceremony was over, I whispered in his ear, "Please don't ruin this for Robbie. Let's just go. We can mingle at the party." I got a nasty look, but he did walk away with me.

We were back in the car before he had a chance to socialize with the parents of Robbie's friends. The few people we ran into on the way to the car, I just said, "It was a nice graduation. I'll see you at the party. We've got to get home and get things ready." Robert was a little irritated, so he didn't say anything. We survived the graduation.

I spent the rest of the afternoon getting things ready for the party while Robert continued drinking to celebrate his son's graduation. Every now and then, I pulled him aside and said, "This is Robbie's day. Please don't ruin it for him."

"I'm celebrating, so leave me alone."

That was all he had to say the couple of times I spoke with him. There was also a time when I overheard Robbie asking him to take it easy on the drinking. Then I thought, maybe, just maybe, I was overreacting; it was a celebration after all. There were only a few people at the house, and it was his family. I left him alone and continued with the preparations.

Teresa and Christine were helping to transport the food to the hall where the party was going to take place. Marsha and Rochelle were in charge of decorating the hall, while Jackie was in charge of babysitting the small children. I had some good friends indeed.

All was going well until the last fifteen minutes of the party. The end of the evening brought about an altercation by Robert, which ended up in the parking lot. Robert was arguing with someone, and when Robbie tried to calm him down, he started yelling at him. Robert went to swing at his son, and if Robbie's uncle hadn't grabbed him, there would have been a father-and-son fight. His uncle said something to him about not fighting his father and giving him respect, but Robbie came back at him with, "You don't know what goes on in our house, so mind your business."

Once the incident was over, I knew I didn't want to spend the night under the same roof with Robert. If

I stayed, I'm sure there would have been an argument, which would have led to a fight. That's how mad I was. He had embarrassed me for the last time, and I was done with the nightly tears. There was no more trying one last time. No more thinking that if I could just get him to an AA meeting, it might help him come out of denial about his drinking. I wanted, needed, and desired to be loved and to give love. There would be no more questions and no more wondering. *It was over.*

Before I left, I spoke to Robbie about what happened and told him that no matter what, I never wanted him to think it was okay to fight his father. He was so angry, but he finally understood and left with his friends.

The good thing about the night was that the grandparents, work friends, and the parents of Robbie's closest friends were gone. Only the memories of pride and joy of the day went with them. The people who remained were the ones who knew about his behavior whenever he was drunk. I couldn't hide his alcoholism from everyone, even though I tried.

Once Teresa and I finished cleaning the hall, I packed a bag and went to her house. Teresa and I stayed up all night trying to figure out the first step toward my new life. I never cried or spoke of any frustration. It was as if the pain was gone, and I was free. The night of the party assured me that the end of the marriage was indeed here.

Since I wasn't a very sociable individual, I knew I needed a friend to help me get back into the dating scene. I thought about asking Teresa to help, but then I realized that it would be better to ask a man. Plus, I didn't want anything to come between Teresa and me if things didn't go well with the matchup. So the question was, who?

I went home the next day to find Robert dealing with a hangover. I had nothing else to say to him. I became more involved with my friends, which kept me out the house. I even spent a few weekends visiting Kyle in Connecticut. By this time, Kyle had settled into a family life with his wife Sandra, his daughter Marie, and his son Lamont. So I went into grandma mode. When I wasn't in Connecticut, the grandchildren would come to me. I would meet Kyle at a halfway point to pick up them up on Fridays and returned them on Sundays.

Robert and I were alone in the house now that Robbie had gone off to college. When he came home from work drunk, I did my best to stay out of his path. Though he tried, his attempts were a waste. As soon as he started, I grabbed my things and left.

Then one day while talking with Kyle on the phone, he mentioned homecoming was coming up at his college and invited me down for the weekend. When I hung up with him, I figured homecoming should be coming up at Cheyney as well. So I gave Rochelle a call to see if she knew when it was. When I hung up with her, I called Teresa to tell her that it was homecoming weekend at the university I attended in a couple of weeks. I decided this WAS where I would get help. Teresa's husband agreed to watch the girls so she and I could attend homecoming weekend.

Two weeks later, on Saturday, I was up by 5:00 a.m., dressed by six, and excited for the first time in a very long time. At least excited about something that was about me and not the boys. I patiently waited until 7:00 a.m. to call

Teresa to see if she was dressed and ready to go. I remember her saying, "Slow down, hot mama, it's too early to go anywhere. I'll see you around ten." So I waited by cleaning the house.

When Teresa finally got there, I was ready to go. She parked and came inside. She looked cute in her jeans and a tight-ass shirt that was sure to have a lot of guys checking her out. That was no doubt the point. I had to change from looking like I was fifty to maybe forty. I initially had on sweatpants. Now my boobs were showing, but not as much as hers, and the tight jeans did make my ass look a little bigger.

On the way there, we talked about who we thought would show up and what they would look like. I hadn't been to Cheyney since I graduated, so I was really looking forward to a day of fun.

Once we arrived, we walked around until I finally spotted someone I knew. It was none other than dear old Rochelle. We hadn't heard from her in a couple of weeks, so we didn't think she would be there.

"What going on, ladies? I went away with a friend and just got back in town this morning. I called you, Miss Cindy, to see if you wanted to go to homecoming, but got no answer. Now I see why."

"This is my debut. I'm here to begin the next stage of my life. By the way, we'll be looking forward to hearing about this trip on Monday."

"So you're saying you finally left Robert?" Rochelle asked with a big smile on her face and her hands clamped together as if she was praying.

"Yes, I am, and I'm glad to see that you are so pleased with my decision. The graduation was the last straw."

"It's about time. Wouldn't you say, Teresa?" Rochelle commented as she gave me a bear hug, lifting me up from the ground.

"Put me down, Rochelle."

"Cynthia just needs to do what makes her happy. That's all that matters to me, but I will say I'm glad she's ready to move on. So come on, ladies, let's go have fun. I have no children to take care of, and I'm not wasting a single minute of this day," said Teresa. She started to chant, "Freedom, freedom!"

"Okay. I know where the gang is, so come on, let's go find you a man," said Rochelle.

With them both on my arm singing "For she's a jolly good woman because she did the right thing" (while stumbling together to find more happy words), we went and sat with some old friends and talked about the good old days.

After a while, I began to get a little bored and decided it was time to go. Things weren't panning out as I had hoped. None of the men in my presence interested me, and no names were mentioned that grabbed my attention. I whispered in Teresa's ear, "I'm going for a walk. You can stay with Rochelle."

"No. Wait, I'm coming with you."

Getting up and turning to walk away, we hadn't gotten two steps when I heard someone ask, "Has anyone heard from Craig White?"

The mention of his name stopped me in my tracks. I couldn't understand why, so I wanted to stay and listen to what they were saying.

So I said, "Teresa, let's sit back down for a bit."

"Why?" Teresa asked as we sat back down.

"I want to hear what they have to say about Craig."

Someone mentioned he was a manager at a book-keeping company called Mascot, Inc. With that information in hand, I turned to Teresa and said, "Okay. Now we can go. I have the information I need."

"What about Rochelle? Cynthia, aren't you going to say bye?"

"So, Rochelle, do you need a ride home? Teresa and I are leaving." All I wanted to do was get home, get on the computer, and find Craig.

"No. I drove. I am going to hang out for a while longer. I will catch up with you tomorrow. Hey, congratulations, Cynthia, and I'll talk to you on Monday, Teresa."

Not much was said on the way home. I dropped Teresa off, picked up a salad from Lucy's, and headed home. When I got in, I went straight up to my room, lay down on the bed, and looked up at the ceiling, trying to remember who Craig was. The ringing of the phone broke my thought process. It was Teresa.

"Hey, girlfriend, what are you doing?"

"I can't stop thinking about Craig. I'm trying to remember who he was, what he looked like, and more importantly, why the mention of his name had such an effect on me."

"I was wondering what you were thinking because you were pretty quiet on the way home."

"I'll get on the computer later to see if I can find him."

"Okay. I was just checking on you. We're going out to dinner, so I will talk to you later."

"Enjoy. Bye."

Later that night, I got on the computer to track Craig down. After a few days, I found someone that I thought could be him. The website for the company he worked for had pictures of their staff members. Not 100 percent sure, I sent an e-mail telling him who I was, where we attended college, the social organization we pledged, and asked if he was a member.

A couple of days passed before I heard from him. When I did, we spent a few weeks just chatting online about our college days. He remembered me as well as some of the men he claimed I was with on campus. I only remembered one of them. Finally, we made plans to meet up. That day would be the start of what I hope would be the best to come for me. He would introduce me to men, and one of them would be my one true love.

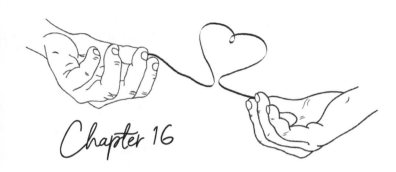

Chapter 16

It was time for me and Craig to meet up. It had been twenty years since I had gone out with another man. What would I wear? Where would we go? I had so many thoughts running through my head. I was nervous and looking forward to our reunion all at the same time. I tried on three, maybe four, outfits before settling on what I thought was the perfect outfit: a blue two-piece skirt set, off-black stockings, and pair of black pumps. A dab of perfume on my neck, a final look in the mirror, and I was out the door and ready for whatever.

I called Teresa to let her know I was headed out to meet Craig and asked if she would talk to me until I reached my destination.

"So what did you decide to wear?"

"My blue skirt set. I'm really nervous."

"Relax and enjoy yourself. I'll call you in a half hour to see how things are going." A few more words, and we hung up.

I arrived a few minutes before Craig, so I parked, got out of the car, and walked around the corner. I sat on a bench that was in front of the art museum near where I parked. It was closed, so I couldn't admire any paintings while I waited. It was around nine that evening, so there wasn't much traffic and just a handful of people moving about.

A car pulled up, rolled down the window, and I heard my name. "Cynthia." His voice was very sexy.

I smiled and said, "Yes. Craig?"

He got out and walked over to me.

As I looked him up and down, he took my breath away. I don't know if it was the heat of the night or the internal warmth I felt running through my body that made me feel passionately hot. I was so worked up from the sight of this man, and then he touched me. For the first time in my life, I felt wetness between my legs based solely on sight. Then the warm touch of his hand on my arm made me feel weak at the knees.

"Where did you park?" he asked.

"What? Oh. I parked around the corner." He probably figured out that I was a little flustered as I stumbled to answer his question.

"Okay. The car will be fine there. Come on, we're going in my car."

He grabbed my hand and walked me to his car. He had a friend with him, so I sat in the back seat. I figured he brought him in case he needed an excuse to cancel our outing, just in case he saw me and wanted an out. Not that I wasn't looking good, but just in case he thought I wasn't his type, this man would be his cover. After all, we hadn't seen each other in over twenty years, and that was a long time. He could have said, "I wanted to call and tell you something came up, but I didn't have your number being that we only communicated via e-mail."

It turned out not to be the case. I had my backup via telephone. My call was to come in thirty minutes after the meeting. Anyway, it wasn't really a date, so it didn't bother me about the friend. We were just hooking up as two college friends hanging out. I was going to tell him sometime during the night what I wanted.

He introduced me to his friend, and then we just started talking about stuff when he reached back and ran his hand up my leg (damn, there was that heat wave again, and it was a good thing I had panties on).

Then he asked, "What do you have on your legs?"

"Stockings," I responded. I wasn't sure why he was asking.

"Girl, if you don't take them damn stockings off..."

I took off the stockings and stuffed them into my purse. I didn't know what to say or do after that, so I just asked, "Where are we going?"

"To a club over in Jersey, so sit back and relax," he said with a smile on his face—and what a beautiful smile it was.

The club turned out to be inside the New Jersey State Aquarium. When you entered the building, the first thing you saw was the dance floor. Straight ahead was the dining area, and off to the left you could go into the area where the aquarium was located.

We sat at a table near the water. It was a nice night, and a wonderful breeze was coming off the river. There was a crescent moon that night, which brought about even more beauty to the atmosphere.

The three of us had a nice time talking and laughing. Craig's sense of humor was very refreshing. The more he made me laugh, the more relaxed I became, and the more I enjoyed the evening. Then there was that moment when he got up to go do something. He pushed back his chair, stood up, reached over, and kissed me on the forehead. That was the first time anyone had kissed me on the forehead since William.

After the initial thought of that intimate moment, I had another thought, and it was *Twenty years with the same man, and not once did he ever leave a table without kissing me.*

"I'll be back in a bit. I need to take care of something."

"Okay. I'll be here." Where else was I going to be, in the river? What a stupid thing to say.

"Keep an eye on her," he said to his friend as he walked away from the table.

When Craig walked away, that was when I really saw how nicely built he was. The stroll he had when he walked away was one of confidence. I sat there thinking about him in a sexual way. I started undressing him in my mind, and by the time he was out of my sight, he was in the nude.

I took a sip from my drink to distract my thoughts, only to begin wondering why I couldn't remember him from school. After all, I did pledge his line, so he should have been in my face daily during that time. Well, the past is the past, and now here I was, staring into the eyes of a very handsome and sexy man. I needed more of a distraction to get this man out my head, so I said to his friend, "I am going over to the aquarium."

"Can I come with ya?" he asked.

"You don't have to watch me. I am a big girl."

"Yeah, you are, but I was told to keep an eye on ya."

"Okay. Shall we go and check out the sharks?"

Since Craig brought his friend with him and we weren't really out on a date, there was no reason why I couldn't flirt with this man. In all the conversations I had with Craig, I never told him I was interested in him. Just that I had gone to the homecoming, and his name was mentioned. That I remembered pledging his line and just wanted to look him up. I was just trying to hook up with friends from my past. Who knows, this friend of Craig's could be my man. After all, he brought him along, and Craig wasn't really trying to get with me. So that meant that his friend and I could hook up. His leaving us alone could have meant just that.

As we walked through the aquarium, he didn't say a word. He just walked along beside me as we checked out the sea animals. So I spoke first. "You're the strong silent type?"

He smiled and said, "Nope."

So we began to talk about the sea animals, and he knew a lot about certain animals we saw. The uncomfortable silence was gone, and we were smiling at each other.

Then I said, "So, do you bring your girlfriend here to impress her with your knowledge of animals?"

"We were here once. To be honest with ya, I learned about them from her."

"Oh!" What else could I say?

Well, so much for the thought of his friend being a love interest. Just as fast as I thought it could be his friend was as fast as I realized it wasn't. We were all out just to have a good time.

We returned to the table before Craig. I sat there staring out at the water, watching the light waves as the water flowed down the river. I was feeling such a sense of peace, and for that moment, I was happy. There was no arguing, no yelling, and no boys to run around town to different activities. Just being out and enjoying a night with a friend. A friend who was stirring up feelings within me that made me feel great. Being with him reminded me that passion existed outside my mental fantasy world other than when I was alone. I didn't need to sip on any coffee tonight to fantasize intimacy from the hot steam and smell.

I turned away from the water just in time to see Craig walking back to our table. It was like something out of a movie I had seen. There he was, walking through a crowd of people, and all I could see was him. It was as if everyone else disappeared. Watching him walk back to the table was rewarding at the onset. He was a fine black man. His hair was cut close, and he was flashing that beautiful smile of his. You could see his strength in his persona.

When he reached the table and stood next to me, he smelled so good. You just wanted to be in his arms and take in his scent for as long as it lasted.

Again, why I didn't notice him in college was beyond me. I wanted to go home with him and give myself to him completely. To deny him of nothing that he desired. *Okay, Cynthia, get it together. Slow down. You know nothing about this man. Sure, you're lusting for him, but he may not be the one.*

On the way out the club, he held my hand as we walked back to his car. "Did you enjoy yourself?" Craig asked.

"Yes. I had a wonderful time."

When we got back in the city and as he walked me to my car, I wanted to ask him if I could go home with him, but thought better of it.

Then he said, "I'm meeting some friends, so I will give you a call soon. Let me have your number. We'll get together again and go out for dinner. Drive carefully, and call me when you get in. Here's my number."

I smiled all the way home. I couldn't wait to get there so that I could call Teresa and tell her about my evening with Craig. I didn't call her on the way because I was too excited, and talking to her may have caused me to lose my focus on the road.

It was about two o'clock in the morning when I got home. Teresa answered on the first ring.

"Were you sleeping?" I asked.

"No, but let me call you back. I'm going in the living room so I don't wake up my hubby."

I could hear him in the background asking, "Who's calling you so late?" She told him I was calling to tell her about my date with Craig.

Teresa called back and listened to me as I told her all about the night with Craig while offering a comment here and there.

"I really had a nice time, Teresa."

"It sounds like you did. Now you told me you were tracking him down so he could help you find a man. Is it turning out that he is the one for you?"

"I don't know. He has caught my attention big time. Look, I'm going to let you go back to your hubby, and I'll talk to you later in the day."

Before hanging up, Teresa said, "With all the excitement I heard in your voice, maybe he could be the one."

"Who knows, Teresa? I don't know him or what his life is about to say that he is or isn't. All I can do right now is revel in the feeling of what is now. Okay, Teresa, we'll talk later in the morning."

"Good night, Cynthia."

I placed the phone in its cradle and dressed for bed.

I woke up that morning from a sexual dream about Craig. I called Teresa later that morning, all excited to tell her about how I had my first sexual dream and how I couldn't wait to see Craig again. In just a matter of twenty-four hours, this man had me feeling like a teenager with a crush. None of the men I dated ever had that kind of effect over me at first sight.

Craig and I went back and forth for a couple of days with e-mails to each other. Then he called to invite me out to lunch. After I got off the phone with him, I called Teresa to ask her if she would go shopping with me to get an outfit for my lunch date.

I met Craig on City Line Avenue in Philly at a restaurant called Houlihan's. Here I was again, just sitting at the table across from him I could feel the passion building up inside. Each time he looked at me, I could feel a tingling sensation moving through my body. Looking into his brown eyes brought warmth to my body. How I wanted to take him home and make love to him over and over again. Without a single touch, how is it that this man was able to bring about a sexual arousal within me? God help me when he does touch my body.

The server came over and asked, "Are you ready to order?"

Craig asked, "Are there any specials on the menu?"

She began mentioning the soups of the day. I heard nothing after "Clam chowder is the soup of the day." I became mesmerized by the sound of his voice as he responded to what she was saying. He had a deep intoxicating voice that took control of my mind. There were moments when I just got lost with a vision of us in the future.

Then I heard him ask, "Cynthia, what are you having? I'm getting the seafood pasta."

"I'll have the crab cakes." Good thing I looked at the menu when we first got there.

We talked more about our college days. That was the only thing we had in common at the time. There was music playing in the restaurant, which pulled us into a conversation about the music of today.

"They don't play music like this anymore," said Craig.

"I know. The young people of today don't know real music, but there are some artists who do come close."

"What does your son listen to?" he asked.

"He listens to rap music. His favorite artist is 50 Cent."

"You need to sit him down and play some old school music to educate him about real artists."

"I will do that." I laughed.

I was enjoying more of his sense of humor while we waited for our food. We laughed and talked about some of the lyrics that were out there with these new artists. The discussions we had were very enlightening. I could listen to him talk all night long.

After lunch, he walked me to my car and gave me a sweet kiss goodbye, and again I found myself smiling all the way home.

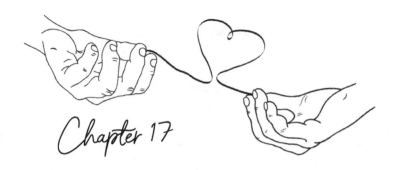

Chapter 17

C raig and I spent a lot of time talking on the phone, seeing each other at the clubs, and occasionally going out to dinner. He would take me to very nice restaurants. When I told him about the places I would go to, he said, "You deserve better than Red Lobster, and I will take you to some of the best places I know."

Then one day, while speaking to Craig on the phone, I told him that Rochelle and I were hanging out, so he invited us to his place. He said he would be home around six. He remembered Rochelle because they had pledged on the same line in college.

The last girl gathering that Rochelle had attended was the Monday after homecoming. I hadn't met with Craig yet, so there wasn't anything to tell the girls. When I did speak to Rochelle, I told her I had been in contact with Craig. She told me she remembered them pledging together, but she couldn't remember his face either. I told her that it was a handsome face, how he had such an amazing effect on me, and that he had a beautiful smile.

When I told her he had invited us up, she wanted to go. On the ride up, I told her that Craig and I had gone out a couple of times, but it was only as friends.

She just said, "Okay," and then she was ready to talk about her. We spent the rest of the ride talking about her latest adventures. When we got there, I realized that he lived in the same development as my oldest sister. I knew my sister's address, but I never really thought about the name of the development. Before we got out the car, I said, "Rochelle, Craig lives over here where my sister lives."

"This is a nice area," Rochelle commented as we got out the car.

I knocked on the door, and when Craig opened it, before he could say anything, Rochelle yelled, "Craig!"

"What's up, Rochelle?"

"I'm good. I didn't know Cindy was talking about you. I remembered your name, but couldn't place you, until now."

"What's up, Cindy? Sit down, ladies. Can I get you something to drink?" We gave him our choice of beverage and sat in the two lounge chairs that were across from the sofa.

"I'm fine. You have a nice home. It has the feel of serenity. It's very cozy and very neat," I commented.

He gave us our drinks, walked over, and sat on the sofa. "Thank you," he said.

There had to be a woman helping him keep his place this way. As I looked around, the décor did fit the man. As neat as it was, it was indeed a bachelor's pad. We talked and laughed about some of the things that took place in the organization we pledged. Well, Craig and Rochelle were on the same pledge line, so I just listened to them as they went down memory lane. We hung out for a couple of hours before leaving. Rochelle had no idea how I felt about Craig at this point. For that matter, neither of them knew. I had only shared my feelings with Teresa, even though those feelings were more about lust than anything else was.

On the ride home, Rochelle commented, "I remember Craig being a ladies' man on campus."

"He's very nice, ladies' man or not." I replied

"I know you aren't trying to hook up with him. From what I know, he would be too much for someone like you."

"What is that supposed to mean?"

"Come on, Cindy, you are too naïve for a man like him. He will eat you up and spit you out. Just from talking to him, I could tell he is still a player. You need a man that only wants to devote himself to you. I hate to disappoint you, girlfriend, but that won't be Craig. You would have to share him with other women, and that is not you."

"You don't know what he's like now. You haven't seen him since college."

"A leopard never changes his spots."

"Well, it doesn't matter, we are just friends anyway. I told Teresa about him and that I just wanted him to introduce me to some of his friends."

"Good. Now a woman like me can handle a man like him. Plus, based on where he lives, I would say he has money, and that, my dear Cindy, is right up my alley."

I listened to Rochelle tell me what she would do with Craig and how she would have him in her bed soon. I wanted to say something to her, but I didn't. I mean, what could I say? Craig and I weren't dating, and I hadn't even told him I was interested.

Typical Rochelle, one minute she's happy I was interested in someone, then when she finds out who he is, she wants him for herself. There's a reason she never became my very best friend.

I dropped her off at home and headed home myself. On my ride home, I called Teresa and told her about our visit with Craig. How Rochelle was all in his face and how I could barely get a word in edgewise. I even told her how Rochelle had decided that she was going to date Craig because I wasn't woman enough to date him.

"So, are you going to tell Rochelle how you feel about Craig?" asked Teresa.

"Not yet, and if she shows up at one of our meetings, please don't bring up my feelings for Craig. Right now my feelings are between me and you."

"Your secret is safe with me. So, it seems as though Rochelle took over the visit. Did you have any of your hot and steamy feelings about him today?"

"From the moment I saw that sexy face of his. Look, I'm almost at home, so I'll give you a call later."

"Okay. Don't let Rochelle put a damper on your day. Bye!"

I spent the rest of the evening thinking about what Rochelle said. I was looking for my soul mate, and if he was a ladies' man, it probably wouldn't be him.

Just as I was getting ready to take a bath, the phone rang. It was Rochelle. "Hello, Cindy."

"What's up, Rochelle?"

"Why don't you give Craig a call and see if he wants to meet up at a club on Saturday?"

"What, you ready to play your hand and wheel him into your web of seduction?"

"Yes, I am."

"Did he give you the impression he wanted to hook up with you?"

"There's not a man around that wouldn't want me. Don't hate the sexy player, hate the game."

"Fine, I'll give him a call. My bath water is getting cold. I'll talk to you later in the week."

Rochelle and I didn't talk every day. Since it was early in the week, I waited until Friday to ask Craig about meeting Rochelle and me at a club. When I did, he said, yes.

I was going to make sure I looked damned sexy that night, so Teresa and I went shopping for the perfect outfit.

On Saturday night, Rochelle and I hooked up around ten. Rochelle was dressed very provocatively. She had on a V-neck white top, a black push-up bra (that had the girls pretty exposed), a mini red leather skirt, and a pair of ankle-strap black sandals. I thought I was looking cute in my short burgundy skirt (that was an inch above my knees) and sleeveless pink silk blouse. My hair was pulled back into a ponytail, and I had on a pair of burgundy strapless open-toe heels.

Craig was standing outside when we got there. "You ladies look very nice this evening," he commented.

Craig leaned in to kiss me on the cheek, but Rochelle stepped in front of me and kissed him on the lips. I could see from the look on his face that he didn't like what she had done.

He grabbed my hand. "Come on, ladies. Let's go inside."

Rochelle flirted with Craig every chance she got. I was a little irritated but said nothing. I sat over on the conservative side of the club and watched people dance while Rochelle spent most of her time on the other side shaking her ass. Every now and then, Craig would show up and ask if I was okay. He made sure I always had a drink and would talk to me for a minute or so before leaving. Every time he saw Rochelle coming toward us, he would leave.

After noticing him doing that a few more times, it made me smile. Yes, Rochelle was my friend, but I was hoping like hell he didn't fall for her. That would make him totally off-limits for me. After all, I was the one who tracked him down, no matter what the reason was.

When we were ready to leave, Craig walked us to our car. This time I got my goodbye kiss.

On the ride home, Rochelle said, "I am no longer interested in Craig." I knew it wasn't her choice to give up on him. I think she realized he wasn't interested in her.

"Why aren't you interested now?" I asked.

"Well, I saw how you were looking at him, and I figured you were interested in him. Every time he looked at you, there was a smile on your face. I never would have said the things I did about him if I knew you were interested."

"I just think he's handsome, and he was always saying something sweet to me that made me smile."

"It's more than that. Anyway, be careful. When he was over on the other side of the club, he was all over the women. That man is a freak, and I think he may be gay [on the down low]. Any man that doesn't pay attention to me got to be a little gay. I would enjoy him in bed, but I respect your feelings, and I wish you the best with him."

"I'm not with him, Rochelle, and you really don't know me that well. You are making an assumption to think I can't be a freak. Besides, I told you I planned on asking Craig to help me find my soul mate. By the way, there is not a gay bone in that man's body."

"Okay, Cindy, whatever you say. I'm hungry. You want to stop and get something to eat at April's Diner?"

"Sure. Since I'm staying with you tonight, I don't have to worry about driving home too late by myself."

We agreed not to talk about Craig anymore, and guess what, it was back to focusing on Rochelle. We got in around two, went straight to bed, and were up by ten. Rochelle was planning a trip to Virginia to see a man she met a few months ago. I dropped her off at the airport, and when I got home, I went back to bed.

Chapter 18

While hanging out with Craig, in such a short time, I began to see a lot in him that I was missing in my life.

The male figures that weren't there: A father, with that stern and forceful way he spoke that made you pay attention (there were times when I couldn't help imagining his children sitting on the floor in front of him, hanging on his every word). The brother, who would be there to protect you if anyone showed you any disrespect. The uncle, who was there to tell you that your father and brother only wanted the best for you, so don't be mad at them.

The passion: it was in his eyes. It made you want to do anything for him. Hell, I wanted to give him the world.

Most importantly, the friendship. Yes, he was becoming my best friend. I could tell him anything and everything.

It was no wonder I was falling in love with him. He had everything I was looking for in a man. I'm not saying he's perfect because he does have his faults. It was just that the good outweighed the bad.

That walk of confidence, his intoxicating voice, and the way he dressed, just to mention a few, were more of the things I admired about him. He brought laughter to me all the time, and he helped me to overcome things in my life that were weighing me down.

For a while, after some of my visits with Craig, I would think about the relationship I had with my husband. It was probably because we were still living together. This was the man had I spent twenty years of my adult life with, and all that I could say about him was that he was a good provider. He was a good man the early part of those years, but always left the raising of the boys up to me. His only input was during football season, and that was just being at the boys' games. Anything else that took place in their lives, I had to make him participate.

I never envisioned things with my husband as I did with Craig. The sex was good for the most part, except his sex drive wasn't that high. I may not have had orgasms, but I was satisfied. I couldn't wait to experience orgasms with Craig.

Chapter 19

Craig and I made plans to go out for breakfast. We went to a quaint little spot in Center City. After the server took our order, he asked, "You want to go to the movies after we finish here?"

"Yes. What are we going to see?"

"Relax. You will know in time."

Then his phone rang. It was a female. She must have wanted to see him because he responded with, "Are you trying to tell me you are available, because I'm not. You should have called me earlier this morning. Sit tight, and I'll call you later to see what's up."

It probably was his girlfriend. Anyway, it was an enjoyable day. We even went back to his house after the movie. We talked and listened to some old-school music. I remember sitting on the floor in front of him, listening to him tell me about some of the places he had traveled to. We got on the subject of vacations when I told him about taking the boys to Disney World. He said that he would take me someplace nice. I wanted to think that we could be in a relationship, but I didn't want to get hurt, so I had to stick with the plan.

When I left that evening, I couldn't wait to get home and tell Teresa about my day. Without fail and after hearing how excited I was yet again, she said, "I'm going to ask you again, is Craig the one you have been looking for?"

This time I said, "Yes, but I can't have him. He is a player just as Rochelle said he was. However, there's no reason we can't be lovers, just until I find a man that has his qualities."

"How do you know he's a player?"

"Didn't I tell you his girlfriend called while we were at breakfast?"

"Okay, don't bite my head off."

We finally hung up. I went and got on the computer. I played some solitaire, responded to some of my e-mails, and even wrote a sexual poem, which I shared with the girls when we got together.

When I spoke with Teresa the next day, she reminded me of our relationship oath. "Cynthia, I just called to remind you of the boyfriend oath, so listen. If a man lived alone and he wanted to see you, even if you knew he had a girl and you weren't crossing any lines being with him, it is okay. He would have to explain any current relationships as noncommitted. If you found out that the man you were seeing was living with a woman or in a truly committed relationship, you pulled out fast. Craig considers himself to be a bachelor. So don't count him out just yet."

Eight months had passed, and I still hadn't gotten around to telling Craig why I tracked him down. It was not that it was a real rush. I had gotten the "fun fever" and wanted to enjoy just being me. Plus, I was still living with my husband. I still had plenty of time to get back on track. Breathe a little before jumping back into the one-on-one relationship.

In the midst of all this, my sex drive was in high gear, and so far, Craig and I were as innocent as two people could be. I don't think he had any idea how much I was lusting for him at this point.

I remember someone told me a while back that men knew—they can tell by the way a woman looks at them. If he knew, he didn't say anything.

I was experiencing feelings I never knew I had, or shall I say the ones that were dominant, such as how passionate I was. There was overwhelming passion, erotic desires, a warm yearning sensation, and downright hot lust. I was almost tempted to have sex with my husband. I went so far as to going into his bedroom, but when I looked at him lying there, I froze for a moment. A rush of negative emotions took over me.

I ran back into my room, angry that I had put some much time into this man, and no matter how hard I tried, I couldn't make my marriage work. I put a CD on by Angie Stone called, "No More Rain." I played it over and over again. I wanted to call Craig, but it was late, so I just turned the music off and cried myself to sleep.

Chapter 20

It was Friday night, and I wanted to go to the club. It would be my first time going out alone. Teresa couldn't go because her husband was on a business trip, and one of her girls was sick. A babysitter was out of the question. Rochelle had plans with one of her male friends, so she wasn't around. I wanted to call Craig to see if he was out at the club, but I decided to move on my own this time. Besides, I wouldn't talk to anyone if he were there. I would be too focused on him.

I put on a black-brown houndstooth dress that came just below my knees, off-black thigh-high stockings, ankle-strap black sandals, and a black blazer (it was early spring, and there was a chill in the air). I thought I was looking good. Heads did turn when I walked into the club.

The last time I went to a club with Rochelle, I stayed over on the conservative side and didn't dance at all. This time I decided to go over on the other side to get my dance on. The music was a little more upbeat. I was standing against the wall, waiting for someone to ask me to dance. For about an hour or so, no one did. Maybe I was standing in the wrong spot, so I moved to another spot.

The crowd was getting larger, and it was getting hotter, so I took off my blazer. Within ten minutes, someone came over and asked me to dance. It wasn't difficult for me to realize that I was overdressed for the club. Now I see why Rochelle had dressed so provocatively. That's what the men wanted. Well, at least on that side of the club. I must have been seen as a woman looking for her cheating man or an old-fashioned girl out of touch, trying to get back on the scene.

Now that I think about it, the night Rochelle and I went out, she mentioned how I should have dressed a little more provocatively. When I asked her what was wrong with what I had on, she just smiled and started talking about something else.

Anyway, after a couple more dances and some lame lines from a couple of men, I had decided that it was time to go home.

I called Teresa when I got in.

"Hey, Cynthia, what's up?"

"I just got in."

"How was the club?"

"It was okay. I was overdressed, but I did get a couple of dances."

"What do you mean overdressed?"

"Let's just say it wasn't club wear."

"Okay. It's late. I'm going back to bed. I need to get a few more hours of sleep before dealing with the girls."

"Alright, I'll talk to you later in the morning, sister girl. I'll stop by to see you and the girls around noon."

We were sitting in the kitchen when I got a call. It was Craig. He was calling to see how I was doing. I told him about going to the club, then he said, "I'll be at club Party Nights on Saturday, if you want to come up."

"Yes. I just have to make sure I have on my party clothes. I was overdressed last night."

"What? Did you have on your mommy clothes?"

"Hey, I would prefer if you label them my work clothes. I'll dress a little better for Saturday."

"You were fine the last time I saw you, for someone coming out for the first time in centuries. All right, Cindy, I have to go. I'll speak with you soon."

Teresa and I went shopping Saturday morning for something to wear. Teresa and her husband had plans for the evening, and Rochelle wasn't anywhere to be found, so I went alone. I was dressed a lot better this time. I wore a pair of blue jeans, a light blue silk top, and a pair of dress boots with two-inch heels.

I didn't see Craig when I arrived, so I just went over to the dance floor. I spent a lot more time out on the dance floor than last week. There was one man I was dancing with who said, "Why don't you turn round for me?" I guess he want to see the whole view. So I did that slow 360 move so he could check out the body.

When we were back face-to-face, he asked, "Aren't you gonna turn round and give me that ass?"

"What?" I wasn't letting anyone feel this ass but Craig.

"Turn that sexy body round, and let me get up on that ass."

This brother was definitely bold. Just as I was getting ready to reply, his phone started to vibrate.

"You should take that call."

Before he could respond, I got the hell away from him. I didn't come out to give some brother a hard-on. Okay, this was my second strike—first the clothes and now the dance moves. I thought, *Let me get the hell off this dance floor.*

I ran into Craig a little while later and told him what happened. He took me over to the other side of the club and told me to have a seat. This was the laid-back side, similar to the other club I went to.

He then said, "I don't know why you were over there trying to run with the young boys. Come with me." He had me follow him around the club the rest of the night like a protective brother. Five of my own, and he was the one who cared enough to protect me. All my brothers did was beat me up or ignore me.

When I was ready to leave, he walked me to my car. Before walking away, he kissed me on the forehead and said, "Do not come to the club alone anymore. Be careful, and call me when you get in."

I called when I got home. He reminded me about not going to the club by myself. Before he hung up, he told me to rest well and that we would get together soon.

Chapter 21

Through all the partying, flirting, and meeting up with Craig, I was still living with my husband. Kyle was living in Connecticut, and Robbie was at Delaware State College. It was just the two of us, and we were living like strangers. I kept asking him to leave, and he wouldn't. I had put so much into my home and didn't want to leave either.

My husband had stopped paying the bills a year before Robbie left for college. I was using my income along with my savings (moving money) to pay the bills. Finally, I asked myself what was more important, this house or my peace of mind? I knew if I wanted to keep the happiness I had now, I needed to move out.

It was March 2001, and I had enough. It was time to exhale. So I started looking for an apartment. Robbie and I spent an entire Saturday looking. I couldn't find anything in my price range. We were on our way back to the house when Robbie asked, "Mom, can we stop at KFC for some chicken?"

"Yes. It's dinnertime." I was tired and not in the mood to cook.

On the way to KFC, I saw another apartment complex. "Hey, let's just check this complex. I promise it will be the last one."

"Mom, you said no more. I'm hungry, and I want to go hang out with my boys."

"I know, but I promise this is the last one."

They had a two-bedroom apartment left. The apartment wasn't too far from my job, and it was in my price range. They were running an end-of-the-month special. They wanted a $500 security deposit, and the first month's rent was free. The other apartments I looked at wanted two months' rent in full, one for the security deposit, and the other for the first month's rent. The other good news was that the application fee was being waived. I completed an application, then we left to go eat.

I decided to wait until my application was approved before I told anyone. I received a call that Tuesday saying it was approved and that I could move in when I was ready because the apartment was vacant. I told Teresa and the girls at our next meeting, which was the next day. I hadn't told my husband. He was on a need-to-know basis, which would be the day I moved out.

Anyway, the girls felt this called for a real celebration, so we went out to dinner. During dessert, the restaurant's staff came over to the table and starting singing:

"Congratulation to you, congratulations to you
You've got your own place and freedom to boot."

This was courtesy of Rochelle, who happened to be around for one of our monthly hangouts. I knew it was her because she disliked him the most because she knew him, whereas the others only knew of him based on the stories about our life that I shared with them.

The following morning, I sat my son down to give him the details that he needed to know about moving day, which would be on Friday.

It was Thursday and my hubby's payday. I still needed money for the U-Haul and a few household items. That night, I invited him into my bedroom. We had sex, and when he went to sleep, I took what cash he had on him. I didn't consider it stealing because he owed me for the couple of years he made me pay all the bills.

That morning while he was getting ready for work, I told him I had taken his cash. He looked at me and just smiled. "Here's the check. Now will you take me to work?" he asked.

Things were turning out even better than I had planned. No sex for almost two years, so I guess he thought we were okay because we got it on. We were all over that bed. I got on top and rode him as if I was on a horse trying to win a race. He flipped me over, and as he penetrated me, he kept yelling, "This is my pussy, this is my pussy!" So now, he was ready to pay the bills again.

Before leaving the house, I woke up my son and told him to get moving on his part for the move. While I was gone, my son went to gather up the friends who were going to help us move. On the way back to the house, I stopped and picked up as many boxes as I could from out back of a nearby market. Not telling my husband I was leaving meant doing all my packing in one day.

I dropped the boxes off, telling the boys what to pack, while my son and I went to get the U-Haul truck. We were able to get everything I wanted moved into the apartment before my husband got off from work. All I took when I left was the living room set, which I had bought a few months earlier, and the boys' bedroom set. They had a bunk bed that separated, so I split the set between the two bedrooms.

Just as I was taking the truck back to the U-Haul company, my phone rang. It was Robert.

"I'm off, and I need a ride home."

"I'm a little busy. You can't get a friend to take you home?"

"No."

"Okay. I'll be there soon. It will be my pleasure to pick you up."

"It would be your pleasure, huh."

"Bye, Robert."

On the way home, he talked about all the things that he was going to do to make things better for us. Did he really think that letting him back in the bedroom meant that we were good again?

Before he got out of the car, I told him I had moved out, and this was the end of a bad marriage. That I hoped he would find someone that he could be happy with and love more than he loved the bottle.

He got out of the car, but not before saying, "I'll see you in the house, and bring me back a six-pack of beer. Use the money I gave you this morning." He didn't believe me until he went inside. He called me on my phone and asked me to come back so we could talk, and I said, "No way."

Teresa came by on Saturday, and we went shopping to get things I needed for the kitchen and bathroom. Rochelle gave me a dining room table set. I admit I was a little afraid since this was the first time I was out on my own in over twenty years. I was beginning another stage in my life that would hopefully be better than the last. I was afraid, but I kept telling myself, "You're not going to depend on anyone to help you, and you will make it."

The first few days, I played my song by Angie Stone, "No More Rain," over and over again. My favorite words in the song were "My sunshine has come."

After being on my own for a couple of days, I thought about Cole, Rochelle's uncle. It was the first time I thought about someone other than Craig. I wondered what he was doing these days, now that I was free to be with him with no stipulations or ties. As long as he didn't want any more kids, we would be okay.

I called Rochelle to see if she had heard from him, but she wasn't home. Each time I tried to reach her, the phone would go to voice mail. Sometimes she stayed at her mother's place, so I decided I would go by there on the way home from work the next day. When I spoke with her mother, she told me that Rochelle had left town, and she didn't have an address or phone number to reach her. Rochelle was good for doing that. Just pack up and leave without telling anyone where she was going. The last time she did this, she ended up in Virginia. Oh well, back to the dating game.

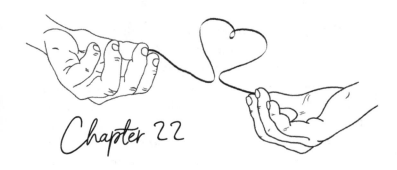

Chapter 22

As I continued with the dating scene, it appeared that all the brothers I met just wanted sex. The few decent ones where living at home with their mother or had three other roommates and were looking for a way out. I figured that out after the third date I had with this one man who was living with his mother. During dinner, he asked, "What do you think about us living together?"

"I don't know you well enough to live together," was my reply. I guess nothing was wrong with it, if that was what you wanted.

When I got home from that date, I called Teresa. She told me she only knew her husband for two months before they moved in together. Then she said, "I understand them wanting to get you in bed. You do have a cute shape now that you've lost the weight since you left Robert. I even pinched my hubby when I caught him checking you out a few weeks ago." Not that she was concerned; it was just a natural thing to do when you catch your man looking at another woman.

"Come on, girl, that man is so into you, I can smell the love he has for you." I intended to find that kind of love someday.

I had dropped down from a size 12 to a size 7 by the time I started going to the clubs. I would work out at home, dancing around in my room, which, by the way, was one of the things I suggested the girls do for their husbands to keep things interesting. I said to the girls at one of our monthly outings, "Ladies, you need to put on the sexiest lingerie you own and seductively dance for your man while he sits in a chair and watch. Put a smile on his face and see what happens." I had seen this suggestion in a movie called *True Lies*. Some of the best ideas can come from a movie.

Anyway, I also joined the Get Fit gym after Craig suggested it to me. He offered to help me pay for it, but I would not accept his money. During my trips to the gym, I did meet a couple of men there whom I went out to dinner with, but again nothing lasted. The closest I got was a man named Raymond, who was okay, until we were out on our fifth date. We had been seeing each other for three months. He told me he didn't want me talking to any men outside of his presence. He didn't believe women should have male friends.

"It's not that I don't trust you, but men can be very persuasive when it comes to getting a girl in bed," he said. I asked him how he thought that would happen since he hadn't gotten any at this point. With a stipulation like that, I had a feeling that this would prove to be an abusive relationship. Been there and done that. That was the last evening I went out with him and accepted his calls. He finally stopped calling after about a month.

Then there was good old Samuel. Samuel lied about having a girlfriend. I found that out when his girl showed up at the gym one day. Wednesday was our workout day. He went on Tuesday, Wednesday, and Thursday, and I went on Monday, Wednesday, and Saturday. We had been seeing each other for four months. Going out to dinner, checking out movies, and of course, there was the gym. I had invited him to my place twice. I felt safer at my place. The one time he asked me to come to his place, I said no. I didn't give it another thought when he never bothered to ask again.

Anyway, at the gym, we would start out walking the track together, and then we would go our separate ways to do our own thing. We would catch up with each other again in twenty minutes on the track. On this particular day, I was already walking the track when he got there. We were finishing our second lap when he stopped walking beside me. I saw him waving to some girl as he bent down, pretending to tie his laces. I kept on walking. When he caught up with me and we were out of her sight, he said, "Cindy, my girl just walked in. I need you to act like you don't know me, and I'll explain everything to you later."

"No problem, consider it done, permanently. That way you won't have to explain anything," I replied as I began to pick up my pace.

"Come on, Cindy, you don't need to be like that. It's not what you think."

I finished by saying, "I know you better move away from me before I go and confront her. Oh, Samuel, please, please lose my number."

I thought it would be fun to torture him a bit, so I continued walking on the track until she got there. I walked side by side with her for two more laps. We talked about what we go through to stay in shape.

I finished my workout, went into the locker room to change, and headed to my car. He was on one of the bikes, which were by the front door, when he saw me leaving. I looked over at him and winked my eye. I was just starting my car up when there he was at my door.

"Cindy, what did you say to my girl?" he asked.

"Wouldn't you like to know? Now back away from the vehicle."

After that encounter, the gym was used as it was designed—for workouts. I worked out and then went home.

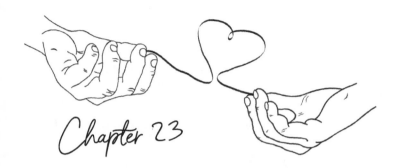

Chapter 23

Craig and I were still hanging out, and yes, I was still lusting after him. The men I was meeting hadn't caught my eye in that manner. So I decided it was time to let him know that I wanted to become a little more than just friends. I began e-mailing him sexual fantasies, and I would make cards expressing how much I wanted him and enjoyed his company. Shall we share a fantasy? It was called "The Office Fantasy":

I am sitting here in my office, thinking about you as an afternoon delight. I called you at work around 11:00 a.m. to ask you to stop by for a lunch at noon. To my surprise, you were standing in the doorway of my office within twenty minutes after I hung up the telephone. I looked at you and smiled. The one thing looking at you always made me do. You walked in and closed the door behind you. Lucky for me, my boss was out of the office, and my staff was at a health benefit meeting that didn't require my attendance.

You came over to my desk gave me a kiss, and then you were closing my blinds. You walked over to me, pulled my head back, and then you said, "Let's have lunch." I pushed the papers off the desk, unzipped your pants, and pulled out your chocolate python and...

Well, I had better stop there. I'm sure you can use your own imagination to complete this fantasy. It can end any way you want it to.

Although he enjoyed reading the e-mails and cards, to a certain extent, they weren't working. All he would say was, "Maybe." I think some of the attraction I had for Craig was that he wasn't easy for me to get. We had been hanging out for two years, and there was no intimacy.

As I said, things weren't moving as quickly as I had intended. I hadn't gotten him in bed yet, so I needed to step up my game. It was time for the face-to-face request.

Craig and I were planning dinner for Monday, the week of Thanksgiving, so I called Teresa so that we could talk it over.

"Okay, Teresa, how do I tell Craig what I want?"

"Just be honest with him. From all that you have told me about him, that is the way to go."

"You're right. I'll do it during dessert, straightforward and to the point."

So on Monday, dressed in a black skirt, pink silk top, and a pair of black boots, I met Craig at an elite restaurant downtown.

He met me at the door and kissed me on the cheek. "How was your ride?" he asked.

"It was okay. Not much traffic."

We ordered dinner and had great conversation. Once we ordered dessert, it was time to make my request. I asked Craig, "Will you help me to find that someone special? And in the meantime, will you become my lover?"

At first, there was that look that said, "Whoa!" Then these fatal words: "I don't think that would be a good idea because it could ruin our friendship," he said.

"No, it wouldn't." Now I thought this because I was under the belief that I could have a sexual relationship with a man and not get emotionally attached. I had a sexual appetite, but wanted to maintain it with one individual during my search for true love. I wasn't going to hop in bed with every man I met, even though I was horny. I wanted to find a relationship that wouldn't be built on sex but real love. So there would be no sex during the get-to-know-you stage. At least not until I felt there would be a commitment.

"I would have to think about it," he said.

"That's all I'm asking," I replied as I stuffed a piece of apple pie in my mouth. Before we departed, I invited him to Thanksgiving dinner.

Thanksgiving dinner turned out to be wonderful. It was my first holiday in my new place. I had all the fixings, turkey, mashed potatoes, macaroni, cranberry sauce, greens, corn bread, stuffing, and dessert.

Craig showed up around 4:00 p.m. He was going to his parents' home from my place. We enjoyed the meal as we sat around the table talking with my son about what he wanted out of life. After dinner, I showed Craig around the apartment since it was his first time there. We looked at pictures, watched a football game, and then he had to leave. I spent the rest of the evening thinking about how much I had missed when it came to the things I wanted because of the path I had taken with my life.

That night, I had another dream about being with Craig. This one was a little different from the other dreams. This time I could feel penetration in my dream. The more I wanted him, the more intense the dreams became. It still amazed the hell out of me the effect this man had on me. It was like nothing I had ever experienced with any other man. It was wonderful and scary all at the same time.

Not to mention the fact that another attraction I had for him was the way he took control. With my marriage, I was in control of everything that the boys did in school, for entertainment, where we went on vacation, and what we would do when we got there. All my husband did was to make sure he had his beer and liquor.

With Craig, I didn't know what we were going to do most of the time when we got together. This is no doubt why I was always in awe of him and the excitement of our time together. The unexpected was often rewarding.

My life was really changing. Craig was contributing to the difference in my life, and it was good. Craig and I had gotten to a point where we were talking every night. In some of our conversations, I would tell him how I would pray for a good man. That even though I knew God already knew what I wanted, I still found myself praying for it anyway.

I hoped that this time around, I would find it all, or at least 80 percent of what I had envisioned in Craig. They weren't big visions, but they were very important to me. More importantly, I wanted to be a part of who he was.

We would enjoy many of the same things, which would make it an easy thing to do. He would be my soul mate. Two souls created by God coming together to form one loving relationship. Someone who made me smile at the sound of his sexy voice. With the break of day and the fall of the night, my thoughts would be of the memories we made together and where everyday duties were a pleasure and not an obligation. Where spending the day thinking of him made life worth living. He would be someone who would take the time to get to know me and had my best interests at heart. Someone I would grow to love more than his eyes could see and more than his heart could feel. He would be the blessing sent from God that was meant to always be.

Chapter 24

Girls' night was still going on once a month. So we got together the day after Thanksgiving. We were still trying to understand this thing called love and its different levels as it pertained to relationships. Jackie, who was on the verge of a divorce, told us that hanging out with us once a month and having these discussions were really helping her. Things were changing, and she and her husband were no longer talking about a divorce. She never wanted one anyway. She told us they were finding each other again. Their love had grown stronger, and they were planning to renew their wedding vows to reconfirm their commitment. They were even talking about having a baby.

I could still see, on occasions, that during these outings, the girls were feeling bad for me. Everyone would be excited as the good news went around the table until they got to me, and I had to tell them about the man that wasn't. Craig was still off-limits with the girls. He was for Teresa's ears only. She wanted me to share with them, but I couldn't. We were just friends. Being the only one without a man wasn't easy. I told them not to feel bad for me because I knew my love would come in time. I told them that I was having fun looking for a prospect. I was learning a lot about the male species. Every now and then, they would ask if they could introduce me to someone, but the answer was no.

The Saturday after Thanksgiving, Teresa and I attended a boat cruise that was hosted by Craig. There were plenty of men to socialize with, but none could hold my attention. All I saw was Craig. There was something about him. I would be talking to a man, and then my mind would drift away. I would start thinking about something we shared together, or he would come into my sight, and I would find myself smiling and lusting for him. His interest in me was still not there, and I knew this, but something was happening to me when I was with him, and I couldn't understand it. I knew that he was becoming an obstacle to my finding Mr. Right because I was falling in love with him. He was giving me all the things I wanted without being told what they were. I guess that was because they were also a part of who he was.

I was still dating, but as I mentioned earlier, the men I would come across thought that sex was top priority in a relationship and that they should establish compatibility right away. So much for learning and enjoying intimacy as you got closer to each another.

Craig and I continued to spend time getting to know each other, having talks that would hopefully assist him with choosing the type of man he would have me meet. Plus, the things we shared and the way he saw how I enjoyed them would help in his choice of prospects.

Then one day after visiting with Craig, as I was leaving, he gave me a hug. Something happened, and before we knew it, we found ourselves in a passionate kiss. Usually when I left from spending time with him, he would always kiss me on the cheek or forehead. From that day on, every so often, we would embrace in a little sexual foreplay. You know, the first base, second base, third base lust game. We were now at that 90-10 friendship. That is, 10 percent of our relationship had become intimate.

When my phone rang and it was Craig, a smile would appear on my face. When I knew I was going to see him, I would feel excited, nervous, and sexually aroused. Then there was the actual sight of him that made me weak to my knees, and no matter what he had on (sweats, jeans, or dressed to the nines), he looked good. The more I desired and admired him, the more handsome he became. It was getting harder to leave him. I hated leaving him just as much as I was falling in love with him.

It was Sunday afternoon, and I got a call from Craig. "You free to hang out with me?"

"Yes. What's on the agenda?" I asked him with a big old smile on my face.

"We can get some lunch and then hang out at my place for a while," he said.

"That sounds good to me. I'll see you in about an hour."

"Okay, Cindy, in a bit."

I was about to call Teresa to see if she wanted to go to the movies. Instead, I was headed to Craig's house. When I got there, we embraced. I didn't want to let go. I wanted to push him into the bedroom and rip off his clothes. It took all my strength to let go. Then he kissed me on the forehead.

We sat around talking for about a half hour before going to lunch. When we got back from lunch, he put a movie on for us to watch. He went to make some popcorn. While he was in the kitchen, I heard him take a call.

When he came back into the room, he said, "Cindy, something has come up, and I need to run out. I have to cut our time short, but I'll call you soon, and we can finish watching the movie."

"Is everything all right?" I asked.

"Just something I have to do," he said.

Trying not to display my disappointment, I gathered up my things, and I smiled as he walked me out to my car. I knew that call was from one of his women. I could hear a little of his conversation as he made one attempt to brush her off when he told her he was a little busy. Obviously she wasn't taking no for an answer, and I got pushed to the curb. I didn't forget that he had other women; I just didn't think one would come between our visit. I was actually jealous. Jealous because I saw that he loved this woman enough to blow me off. She was his priority. Then I got a little irritated at the fact that I had never felt a jealous emotion about my husband.

Things were getting away from me. I thought I had control of my path. I thought I could really be involved with Craig without a desire for more than sex. Reminding

LUCINDA JOHNSON

myself that he was just a good friend who was there to help me find my true love would keep me focused. I kept fighting it, but the more I fought to control my emotions, the more I felt love for him.

On my way back home, I called Teresa to see if she wanted to hang out. I went straight to her house. I finally admitted to her that I thought Craig was my soul mate. The man who I wrote the poem for called "Oh Love." I couldn't understand why I felt he was my soul mate. I just did. Even though we were from two different worlds, I wanted to be with him every day so that I could take care of him. What was happening? Here I was falling in love for the first time in my life, only it was with my best friend.

I didn't know what to do with these feelings. Run before I got in too deep, or stay and continue to enjoy what was for as long as I could. When I asked Teresa to help me get a grip, she replied by saying, "You are having so much fun. You are enjoying life for a change. I can't remember ever seeing you this happy without it being something about your boys. We both know he has other women, so you may not get what you want with him. If you still want him to introduce you to some men, then mention it to him again and go with the flow. You never know what will happen if you give up."

She was right. I had devoted my entire adult life to my boys, and I was taking in the abuse my husband was dishing out, in spite of what it was doing to me emotionally. I had joy in my life now.

After venting with Teresa, I looked at her and said, "Okay, girl, back to the ground rules," with a cheerful smile.

"He is not your man, he is not interested in you as a partner, and he is here to assist with your search for your love. He won't be your soul mate, but the next best thing. Now get out there and find you some prospects." You know, that "check yourself" conversation.

It was Friday night, so Teresa got her husband to watch the girls, and we went to the club. I actually had a nice time. I met a few men, one in particular whose name was Darren. Before we left, I gave him my number.

Later during the week, Craig called to invite me out to dinner. After the last invite, I wasn't sure if I should go, but I got that warm sensation I get when I hear his voice, and I couldn't say no. Teresa and I went shopping for something nice to wear. I even brought a black teddy just in case it was the night to embrace in lovemaking. After shopping, we went for lunch, and of course, we spent time talking about Craig. I told her that I told Craig about Darren. She asked me why.

I said, "It's because he is my advisor, and he is supposed to be helping me find Mr. Right. He's not for me, no matter how much I want to be with him. Telling him about my dates will help me get past my feeling for him. I hope. Most of all, Teresa, it was to see if he would get jealous."

"Did he get jealous?"

"Only a little bit. I could hear it in his voice when he asked me questions about Darren."

"Then maybe he has feelings for you as well."

"That would be from your lips to God's ears."

The evening with Craig began with a romantic dinner at a very luxurious restaurant. As I looked at that handsome face from across the table, I felt love. Every now and then, he would feed me from his plate, and that was turning me on. It was something I always thought was a sweet, intimate exchange between lovers. I began to undress him with my eyes, and as my thoughts began to run wild with passion, I could feel the warmth flow through my body.

He was wearing a navy blue shirt that buttoned down the front, and I was unfastening each one of them slowly as I looked into his beautiful brown eyes. His shirt completely open, I began to rub my hands all over his sexy chest. I could even imagine how warm his body would feel to the touch of my hand.

In the middle of my thoughts, the server came over to the table and distracted me. She wanted to know if we would like dessert. I simply said, "No, thank you, and please bring the check."

Again, he walked me to my car, gave me a passionate kiss, and said in that sexy voice of his, "See you soon, baby girl."

There I was having my first passionate fantasy in public. It was different from just writing them. It became real because he was fulfilling yet another fantasy I had written.

I called Teresa on the way home that night and told her all about it. She said, "Girl, I've got to go. You have put thoughts in my mind, and I need to be with my hubby. Talk to you tomorrow."

Craig called on Sunday to see if I wanted tickets to see Erykah Badu in Atlantic City. He couldn't go, so the tickets were mine. I called Teresa, of course, to see if she could go. Later that night, we met him downtown for the tickets. We met him at the spot where it all began. This was the second time Teresa had met him. She walked over and whispered in his ear. He looked at me and smiled. He gave me a kiss and left.

"What did you say to him?" I asked Teresa.

"I just said, 'Thank you for making my girlfriend happy,'" she replied.

The concert was great. On the way home, I called Craig to say thanks. He was really contributing to the fun I was having as a single woman. Once again, before I went to bed, all I could do was thank God for bringing us together.

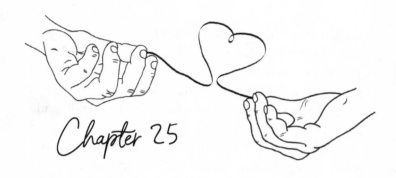

Chapter 25

I knew that I was putting too much time into Craig. I needed to go out and begin looking for love with someone else. Yes, Craig was adding to my happiness, but I still had to accept the fact that he was not going to be the man that I wanted. Not in the way that I needed a man to be, which would be someone who wanted a one-on-one relationship.

Craig hadn't introduced me to anyone as of yet, so Teresa and I decided to go back to the club. On Wednesday, we went shopping for something sexy to wear. I went for a mini red leather skirt and a sleeveless silk blouse. Teresa got a sleeveless light blue dress.

On Friday, we headed to the club. There were still no prospects. When we got back to my house, the two of us sat and talked for a while. I checked my messages and noticed that Darren had called.

Teresa couldn't help commenting on why she thought I should give him a call. "He is single. Craig is the only reason you haven't given him a chance. If you keep comparing every man you meet to Craig, you're never going to be with anyone. I understand that you believe that Craig is your soul mate. Because you can't handle being in the type of relationship he offers, you have got to move on, or at least stop spending so much time with him."

"I hear you, Teresa. Some things are easier said than done."

"Try a little harder, or go after Craig. I need to head home. Remember what I said."

"I will. Drive safely, and call me when you get home."

After getting dressed for bed and settling down with a glass of red wine, I called Darren. We had spoken candidly for a while, and then Darren proceeded to tell me how he would please me if we made love. There it was— sex, sex, sex. I decided to let him tell me what he would do. The more he talked, the more Craig began to pop into my head. I was starting to vision Craig doing the sexual things Darren wanted to do. My mind must have drifted a little too far because his voice had transformed into Craig's voice, and the lustful thoughts had gotten out of hand. I ended up calling Darren by Craig's name. The only thing that brought me around was hearing Darren yelling, and it wasn't because he was having an orgasm.

He was yelling, "Who the hell is Craig?" Then I heard him bang down the phone.

I wanted to call him back to apologized, but decided to wait until the next time we spoke. I stayed with my vibe and dreamed about Craig.

I woke up and realized I needed a week off from the world of dating and Craig. I threw myself into my work. I worked at two locations with my company, so staying busy was not an issue. I would go in early and worked late. I called Teresa on Friday to let her know I was going to Atlantic City (AC) for the weekend and would give her a call when I got back. I went there often, and it was relaxing.

On the way home on Sunday from AC, I called Teresa to ask if I could come over. First, we talked about my strolls on the boardwalk, swimming, and how I only had dinner in my room. I mentioned that I did a little flirting, but that nothing really came of it. I also told her that I only thought about Craig once, but she knew I was lying. She said she could see it in my eyes. She asked if I had spoken with him, and I told her that he called Saturday night. We spoke for a while, and I invited him up, but he had something to do. I thought about calling Darren, but I never got around to doing it.

Then Teresa asked, "Cynthia, what is it that you want, and do you really think Craig can give it to you? Better yet, do you see him giving up his lifestyle for you?"

"No, I don't see him doing that, but I'm falling for him nonetheless. You know that I asked him to help me find my life partner, and we still haven't talked about us as a couple. Okay, what was the rest of your question? Oh yeah, what do I want? I want a man that will love me, of course. A man that makes me laugh, sing melodies to me, takes the time to figure out who I am, and will help me fulfill most of my fantasies—in and out of the bedroom. I also want a man who comes from a loving family. Most importantly, a man who can make the smallest of things we share together feel like the biggest things we share. That can be something as simple as enjoying movies at home."

"You think Craig can give you these things?"

"He has already begun to do some of them. That is why I'm falling in love with him. Now, I hope I have answered all of your questions. Now, I would like to move on to the task at hand. Finding another man who will give me what I want. If you can't be with the one you want, you have to find the next best thing. So I'm going to give Darren a shot. Is that what you want to hear? I'm tired. It's time for me to head home. I will call you tomorrow."

"Girls, come say goodbye to Auntie Cynthia."

During the early part of the week, I got a call from Darren. First, I told him I was sorry for what happened the last time we spoke. We then made plans to hook up on Thursday. I was going to give him another chance to see if he could keep me from thinking about Craig. To see if he could be the man I desired. If I could spend an entire date without Craig popping into my head, it would be a good sign.

It was date night. I went to Darren's place where we listened to some R&B music, and I entertained him with some seductive dancing. When I noticed that he was enjoying it a little too much, if you get my drift, I ended it. We walked around the corner and got some takeout Chinese food and a movie from the video store. The movie was called *Love Jones*. It was a good movie. After a few obstacles, the two main characters got together. They made love, and that morning, he got up and cooked her breakfast. You can say he woke up feeling good.

Being a sucker for love, I cried and thought it was the sweetest thing. Darren invited me to stay, but I told him I had an early morning meeting and needed to get home. When he went to kiss me, I pulled back. It was as if a magnet pulled me away from him. So I bent over and kissed him goodbye on his cheek.

"Damn, baby, that's all I get? A kiss on the cheek like I was somebody's kid?" he asked.

"Yes, and don't look at it as a child's kiss, but as a term of endearment."

Darren was nice, but I don't think he's going to be the one. We enjoyed each other's company, but he just didn't do it for me, so all I saw was friendship. Plus, he didn't keep Craig from entering my thoughts. He had none of the things I told Teresa about that I wanted in a relationship. The more men that kept hitting the reject pile, the more attractive Craig became.

Craig and I were still seeing each other, and he was still fulfilling my dreams. I couldn't distance myself from him. Yes, I had it bad for this man. It was not even about the lust anymore. He was just the one. I was headed into unfamiliar territory. If I tried to work within the boundaries of this relationship, would I be able to handle it with this man? To be with a man who has other women? I don't think I'm selfish, but at the same time, because of the way he makes me feel, I would want to be with him as much as I could. It would be hard, not knowing when I could see him, from one day to the next. Each visit trying to get all that I could when we were together. I'm not saying that I'm not a strong woman, that I couldn't do it if I had to, but I am demanding, and I'm learning that I could be a very jealous woman.

I just don't know anymore. There would be nights when I would cry on Teresa's shoulders, trying to understand what was happening. Just as I did years ago, when I was lost and confused about my family.

Why haven't I ever felt this way about my husband? I can't believe—no, I don't want to believe that in the twenty years we were together, none of these feelings surfaced. He wasn't always the person he became at the onset of our fail marriage.

What am I going to do? Why does my soul mate belong to others? He's not showing any real interest, and I'm in love with him. Well, at least not that I could see. Teresa would tell me to have faith and be patient. There has to be a reason why God sent this man to me. Nothing is really of our own doing. Everything happens for a reason.

Chapter 26

I hadn't seen Craig for a few weeks, and I was missing him like crazy. I decided to stay away. We just talked on the phone. When he wanted to hang out, I told him I had plans. He never asked why, so I didn't have to give a detailed reason.

A couple more weekends at the clubs, and there were still no worthy prospects. The men I met were idiots. The lines they would run down weren't going to get them a date, much less sex.

I remembered one night at the club, a man approached me and said, "You have beautiful eyes, and they are telling me that you want me."

"Is that so," I replied. "I thank you for the compliment, but the rest of what you said is totally incorrect. Do you use that line very often, and does it really work for you?" Of course, he turned and walked away.

Then there was another time when a man who stood next to me at the bar said, "If I throw this water bottle in that trash can from here [which was about three feet away], will you give me your number?"

Of course, the answer was no. The only positive thing about him was that he was drinking water. Well, maybe. Was it because he was trying to sober up before he headed home, or was he a recovering alcoholic?

When the lines didn't work, they would politely walk away and look for their next victim. I decided to give up the club scene for a while. Teresa and I would use our nights out to go to the movies or dinner and just talk about life and love.

Darren was still calling, so I decided to go out with him again. This time I decided to make it a double date, so I called Teresa to see if she and her husband wanted to do a double date on Friday. She said she would ask her hubby and get back to me. She called the next day and said, yes, so we went shopping for outfits. Teresa picked up a backless red linen dress and a pair of red-and-white slip-on stilettos. I got a T-strap black linen dress with black-and-white ankle-strap stilettos. We went to the nail salon to get manicures and pedicures. We then had lunch and, before departing, decided to meet at my place around seven.

We went to Red Lobster for dinner. Teresa and I ordered Long Island ice teas, and the men ordered beer. We also ordered our meals before the server left to get the drinks. We talked about the weather, the kids, and a few movies that we had seen while waiting for our food. When the food arrived, I could see right away that Darren needed a lesson in table manners. Teresa noticed it too because she kept kicking me under the table.

Her hubby began to feed her from his plate, and Darren commented by saying, "They always want what we ordered." Her husband just looked at him and smiled.

Darren asked, "You want to taste my food?"

I just shook my head and said, "No, thanks."

When the server came back to see if we wanted dessert, everyone ordered something but me. Teresa and I excused ourselves from the table to go the ladies' room. We were in there laughing about Darren's table manners. How he slipped the silverware out of the napkin and left it on the table. How he ate his food, as if the server was going to come back too soon and take his plate away. How he was licking his fingers instead of using the napkin. He couldn't even understand the intimate sharing of food between couples.

We returned to the table just as the dessert was being served. Twenty minutes later, we were on our way to the car. We had gone to the restaurant in Teresa's car, so she dropped us off at my place, and they headed home to relieve the babysitter.

I called her an hour later to let her know that Darren had left, that I had spoken with Craig, and he invited me up.

"What brought the visit on?" she asked.

"I told him about our double date. Then I mentioned how I wanted to come over and show him the sexy lingerie I was wearing. He said to come on up."

"Okay. Be careful, and call me in the morning with details. Bye."

I spent almost two years trying to get in his bed, and now it was finally going to happen.

I decided I was going to do this right. So since it was a cool fall night, I just put my trench coat on over my lingerie. Here I was, going to his place dressed like someone in a scene from a movie I saw called *Boomerang*. She had gone to see her man, and all she had on under her coat was lingerie.

I packed an overnight bag and was on my way. The drive was a little nerve-racking because I was worried about being pulled over.

When I got there and took my coat off, Craig smiled and said, "Good thing you didn't get pulled over."

We had a drink, sat down, and talked for a while. Then he grabbed my hand and walked me into the bedroom. He was gentle, passionate, and loving. He had me in positions I only saw in movies. I lost count of the orgasms. By the time I fell asleep, I was completely satisfied.

The next morning, after having sex again, he offered to take me out to breakfast. He left the room, but when he returned, he told me to stay in bed and that he would fix breakfast. It was a very nice breakfast. He made omelets, grillers, potatoes, toast, and served it with hot tea and juice. The entire time spent with him was wonderful and definitely worth the wait. The visit reminded me of that movie I watched with Darren called *Love Jones*. There this man was, being wonderful and bringing me joy.

Now, I usually called Teresa to tell her about my visit with Craig, but this time when I got home, I just wanted to stay in the moment. I didn't want any of that "be careful, you know the deal" speech. Just to revel in the moments and hours that followed. Every time I thought about us making love, I would get all flushed with a big old grin on my face.

He sent me an e-mail the next day saying, "Thanks for the love." It took me a week to get over what I was feeling from that night.

Teresa called Saturday evening to see how the night went with Craig. As we talked about it, she was just as happy for me as I was. Then she asked if I wanted to go to the club. The girls were visiting their grandma, and her husband was on a business trip. I told her I would pick her up around ten.

I called Craig to see where he would be hanging out. Teresa and I met up and headed to the club. Craig and I spoke off and on throughout the night. Before he left the club, he said, "Cindy, we'll do more exciting things together, and we'll go out to dinner later in the week." He gave me a kiss, then said, "Give me a call in a couple of days. I want you and Teresa to head home. Be careful on the road, and call me when you get in."

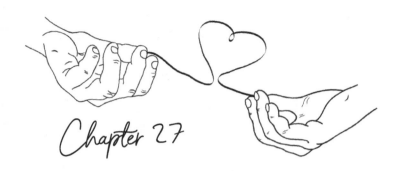

Chapter 27

The Christmas season was closing in on me, and I hadn't gotten any gifts yet. I needed to go shopping, so I called Teresa to see if she still needed to get gifts. She still had a few things to pick up for the girls, so we met up at the mall around noon. After purchasing holiday gifts, a few outfits, and some lingerie for Teresa and me, we went over to Macy's so I could get a gift for Craig. I got him a set of serving trays. I thought it would be a nice holiday gift, and it was something that he could use.

Once I got home from the mall, put my stuff away, and wrapped my gifts, I became bored. I didn't know when I would see Craig again, so in the meantime, because Darren kept calling and asking to see me, I figured there was no reason why we couldn't try to be friends. If I desired male company and Craig wasn't available, Darren could fit the bill.

So I went up for a visit. What started out as a nice evening ended on the wrong foot. When I got there, we went to get a cheesesteak and some fries from the corner steak shop. During dinner, we watched a kung fu movie. They were Darren's favorite kind of movies.

After dinner, we listened to some music. Darren decided he wanted to dance for me. He wanted to pretend he was a stripper, so he began to strip. The more he took off, the more turned off I became. I didn't want to hurt his feelings, so I just watched. Clothes really do hide a lot. He had no muscles at all. I was getting ready to tell him to stop when he dropped his boxers. Well, that was it—there wasn't going to be any lovemaking between the two of us, and that is all I'm going to say on the subject. Well, maybe just that if length doesn't matter, width should.

He was getting ready to say something when his phone rang.

I quickly said to him, "You better get that, could be important."

"I'll let the machine pick up and call them back later."

"Just answer the phone, Darren." All I wanted to do was get the hell up out of there. The opportunity arose, but not in my favor. He took the call, and when he hung up, he had this scared look on his face.

"What's wrong?" I asked.

"It's my girl. She said she's downstairs."

"Okay, I will get my stuff and leave."

"Don't go. She's only going to be here for a minute. She said she just wanted to stop by before going to work to give me something."

"That's cool, but I'm leaving."

"No! You can hide downstairs in the bathroom on the second floor."

This man had lost his mind if he thought I was going to do that. He lived in a three-story house that was turned into an apartment.

"I'm walking out the front door. You will have to explain yourself to her if she asks who I am. You can always say I don't know and that I must have been visiting someone on the second floor. This is your problem and not mine."

As I picked up my purse, the phone rang again. This time she was calling him back to say she was just playing. At this point, it didn't matter. Darren had told me he was single. That he had no girlfriend and no children. He lied to me, and that became the determining factor as to what kind of relationship we would have. We would definitely be just friends. In my book, lying was not going to be a part of my new relationship. I had too much of it in my past relationships.

On my way home, I called Craig, and I told him about my visit with Darren. He listened to the whole story, and then he proceeded to remind me how lucky I was that I didn't get into a fight. That we didn't have to get the police involved. He also said I needed to work on being a better judge of character.

I responded with, "That's why I asked you to introduce me to some of your friends. I knew that I wasn't very good at judging people. My husband turned out to be a prime example of that."

Frustrated again, I decided I needed to take a break from men, so I decided to spend the weekend with my grandchildren. They were always a great distraction. It just seemed like no one was good enough. Even when I lowered my standards a little, and still no one rose to the plate. It just convinced me even more that the man meant for me was Craig.

I called my son Kyle to ask him if I could have the kids for the weekend. He was glad to hear from me. It gave him and his wife a well-needed weekend. We agreed to meet halfway, so our pickup point was at a New York rest stop. We agreed to meet back up on Sunday around seven that night.

Once I picked them up and we were back in the city, my granddaughter wanted to invite a couple of her friends over, which included Teresa's girls, to spend the night. With her friends there, it gave me more time to spend with my grandson without my granddaughter getting jealous.

I thought that maybe, if I do something nice for someone, something good would happen for me. Kindness begets kindness. So after some deep, deep, soul-searching, I called my estranged husband and told him I had our grandchildren. I told him if he wanted to, he could come over and spend time with them.

When he got there, our grandson didn't want to have anything to do with him. The scent of alcohol was reeking through his body, and I guess the odor bothered him. I was angry and was more than ever convinced I made the right decision in leaving him. At that moment, as if I hadn't in the past, I realized that I had no more feelings left for him. For some reason, I thought that maybe we could coexist as friends. I didn't really hate him but hated the person he had become, and all I wanted was my freedom.

It was happening as I stood there looking at him. The last of my feelings just drained away, like blood from a cut. Once it stopped, it was over, and you just waited for the healing to begin.

I showed him to the door, and that was the last I saw of him. I began to question my decision to tell him. "Cynthia, Cynthia, what were you thinking by inviting him over? You couldn't come up with another good deed?" I just put my face in my hands and shook my head.

On Sunday, I returned my grandchildren to their father. I asked Robbie to ride with me, but he had other plans. I didn't want to take that ride alone, so I called Craig, and he was also unavailable. It was just my grandchildren and me.

When I got back home, I went and sat with Teresa. Her husband was home, so the three of us sat around and talked about the old days, danced to some hip-hop music, drank wine, and feasted on junk food. For those few hours, Craig was off-limits. I could talk about anyone but him. I had too much to drink, so I stayed the night.

Darren had called all weekend, but I didn't return any of his calls until Tuesday. He claimed he had broken up with his girl. They got into a big fight about what she did the night I was there. He said he was a free man and wanted to be with me. He tried to convince me, with all he could come up with, why we could be more than friends. Once again, I told him that we could only be friends at this point. He didn't like that, so he hung up on me. I took that to be the end of that saga.

When I got off the phone, I called Teresa to see what she was doing. She invited me over for dinner. We sat out on her deck enjoying a glass of wine while a chicken casserole was baking in the oven. It was a rainy summer evening, and the breeze from the rain felt good. I felt the serenity of the night while sitting there with my very best friend.

We were talking about going to see a play that was in town when my cell phone rang. It was Craig. He was calling to see if I was free for dinner tomorrow. I told him yes, and he said he would be by to pick me up around eight.

When I hung up, Teresa said, "Oh, Cynthia, it's truly amazing the way that man affects you."

"What are you talking about, Teresa?"

"First, you got the biggest grin on your face, just from seeing his name on that phone, and then your eyes lit up like a Christmas tree when he began to speak. You are whipped."

Teresa's husband had joined us just before the phone rang. He said, "Honey, I agree with you. Damn, Cynthia, you got it bad. If that man let you get away, he's a fool. Teresa told me about you and Craig. He's the one you are looking for. Why aren't you trying to get with him?"

"He is not interested in me in that way. We are just good friends, with a little something on the side."

"Okay, sister girl, you keep telling yourself that. Let's go in to eat," Teresa said as she shook her head.

I left an hour after dinner. I thought more about my relationship with Craig, so I called Teresa and told her that I was going to go after him. I was going to make my feelings known to him and see what happened. I was ready to take the risk.

The day of the play, Teresa's daughter got sick, and she couldn't go. I called Craig to see if he wanted to go.

FINDING A SOULFUL LOVE

After the show, I would tell him how I was feeling about him.

"What's the name of the play?" Craig asked.

"*What's on the Hearts of Men?*" I replied.

"Not interested. Why don't you give Darren a call and see if he would be interested in going. It's okay with me if you go with him."

I wanted to ask him why would it be okay with him, but I just left it alone. I called Darren. First, I asked him if he was over himself and ready to accept the fact that there was only friendship between us. "I guess I have to be," was his reply.

I told him I had tickets to a play, what time it started, and asked him if he wanted to go with me. I told him what it was, and he said yes.

On the way to the play, Rochelle called. "What's up, Rochelle? You back in town?"

"Yes, and I wanted to let you know that my uncle Cole is coming to town tonight. His mother is in the hospital for some type of surgery."

"Okay. What's going on with you, and where did you disappear to this time?"

"I've been home for a week now. I was in Florida. I was just getting around to calling you when I heard from Cole. What better phone call can you give a friend than to tell her that an old love is in town?"

"Well, I'm glad to hear that you're back, and I will call you in a little while. I'm on my way to a play with a friend."

"Okay. Talk to you soon."

The play was good, but it wasn't worth the cost of the tickets. After the play, Darren wanted us to go to his place, but I told him no, so he asked me to drop him off at a club. On my way home, I called Rochelle to talk about Cole. I told her that I would come by to see her tomorrow afternoon.

With Cole in town, I had a chance at dating someone. Cole would be someone who could help me get over what I was feeling for Craig. I still believe Craig to be my soul mate, but under the circumstance, I had to settle for the next best thing.

Cole and I had good times together. It had been years since I had heard from him, so we would have a lot of catching up to do. Cole and I had met one more time, a month after he left. Cole sent me a ticket to come see him. While I was there, he still tried to talk me into moving with the kids down south, but I wouldn't go. During that visit, we played board games and, of course, a little one on one. He took me around the army base to meet some of his friends. It was a taste of what could be if I wanted it. But I couldn't grab that rainbow. It wasn't within my reach. I tried to touch it by standing on my tippy toes, but still, no luck. Maybe now I had a chance with Cole. The boys were grown and living their own lives.

When I got to Rochelle's house that afternoon, she was on the phone talking with Cole. He was at the hospital visiting his mother. She gave me the phone so I could speak with him. He said it was good to hear my voice, and he wanted to spend some time with me. So we made plans to meet later that night.

However, twenty minutes later, he was at Rochelle's door. The hospital was nearby. I chalked that up to being a good sign. He was eager to see me. We spent the afternoon talking about old times. We talked about how he wished I had taken him up on his offer to move to South Carolina. I reminded him why I didn't and told him if things were different, I would have gone with him in a heartbeat.

Then he dropped the bomb. He was married with five kids ranging from ages six to thirteen. He was doing contract work and was away from home a lot. He stayed in hotels during the week and went home most weekends. The kids were homeschooled by his wife.

Then he said, "I think about you from time to time."

"That's nice to know. Although I don't think your wife would like it if she knew that. I asked Rochelle about you, but she never told me you were married, just that you had three kids. You have been busy."

"We got married when the third kid turned six. I was going away on a tour of duty for a year, and I wanted to make sure the kids were going to be okay. The last two boys are twins. We were planning to separate when she told me she was pregnant. So how have you been?"

"Still only two boys, but I left my husband, and I have my own apartment now."

"I would like to see your apartment if I can see you again later tonight."

"Sure. Just give me a call when you're ready to come by." I gave him my number and headed home. Cole went back up to the hospital. I hadn't heard from Cole by nine, so I decided to go to the club. I called Teresa to ask her if I could stay over if I went to the club. It would be a shorter drive for me. We had plans for tomorrow, so it made sense for me to stay. We were going to lunch and then to the movies. She said she would leave the key under the welcome mat. I started to call Craig to see if he was out, but decided to do this on my own.

The club was packed as usual. There were two areas in the club. I went over to the bar, ordered a glass of red wine, and as I was getting ready to pay for it, I heard a man say to the bartender, "I'll have a draft beer and take out for the lady's drink."

As I thanked him for the drink, I looked him up and down. He was around 6'2", bowlegged, and had the deepest dimples I had ever seen on a man. He was handsome and had a nice smile. The only difference in his smile and Craig's was that I saw a sparkle in Craig's eyes when he smiled. I know, I know, I shouldn't be comparing men.

"My name is Barron, and yours?"

"Cynthia."

"Are you alone tonight?"

"Yes, and what about you?"

"I'm stag tonight. My hanging-out partner had other plans tonight. It works out well for me because that means I can spend the evening with you, if you don't mind?"

"I don't mind."

"I've been coming here for the past few Saturdays, and I've never seen you in here."

"I'm usually here on Fridays. I felt like getting out tonight."

"Well, I'm glad you did. You look very nice."

"So do you."

"Now that you're finished with your drink, would you like to dance?"

"Sure."

He took my hand and led the way to the dance floor. We were on the dance floor for about three songs when I asked him if we could take a break. Our seats at the bar were taken, so we sat on the sofa.

"Can I get you another drink?"

"Yes, vodka and orange juice, please."

"Okay. I'll be back. Don't you sneak off on me."

"I won't." Barron had peaked my interest.

Okay, Cynthia, he seems very nice, and he looks good. Let's see what else he has to offer this evening. Should I ask him if he's single? No. Let's get through the night. All will come in time. There goes my mind working overtime.

"Here you are." He handed me the drink with a smile that showed his deep dimples. "So, Cynthia, do you come here alone?"

"No. I'm usually with my girlfriend. I decided to come out at the last minute, and she couldn't get a sitter."

"I guess you don't have that problem?"

"No. My boys are grown. No babysitter needed. What about you?"

"I have an eight-year-old son who lives with his mother. Before you ask, we are separated. Five months now."

"I see." At that point, I took a sip of my drink, wondering what my next move would be. "Excuse me, I need to go to the lady's room."

"Did I say something wrong?"

"No. I'll be back."

I needed to call Teresa. I didn't know if I should pursue the conversation about his relationship with his wife. I didn't want to be involved with him, not knowing what it was. So I wanted to see if she thought I should. In the lady's room, I gave her a call.

"Hello, Cynthia."

"Peace, Teresa. I'm here at the club, and I've met this nice man. Things were going fine until he mentioned he has an estranged wife and an eight-year-old son. Estranged as in five months. Girl, there can be baby mama drama in this relationship. So, should I ask him what happened, or should I just go with the flow and wait to see how things play out?"

"I would wait. Change the conversation and stay away from relationship questions. Dance and talk about everything but nothing." In case you're wondering, that statement means to have small talk.

"Okay. I have to go now."

"Wait!" Teresa yelled. "If he wants to get with you again, he will ask for your number. Make sure you ask for his. We'll talk in the morning. Later."

"Okay. Peace."

I hung up and headed back to Barron. Before I had a chance to seat down, he wanted to go back out on the dance floor. We danced for a couple of more songs before we sat back down. As Teresa had suggested, we immersed ourselves in small talk. After about another hour, I was ready to go.

"Barron."

"Yes."

"It was nice meeting you. I'm going to say good night."

"It was nice meeting you as well. Can I get your number? Maybe we can go out to dinner soon."

"Sure. We can swap numbers. I'll be away for a week, so I'll give you a call when I get back in town."

We swapped cell phone numbers, and he walked me to my car. He mentioned how nice it was to meet me again as he stood there until I got in my car and pulled away. I thought about him on the way to Teresa's house. Was he telling the truth about being separated? If so, what type of relationship did the two of them have at this point? Did I really want to get involved in a relationship with small children in the picture? Well, at least I didn't think about Craig tonight. That was a first for me in a long time.

When I got to Teresa's, I moved around as quietly as I could. It was a nice night, so I got a glass of wine and sat out on the deck. The light breeze of the night moved the leaves on the trees. The lightning bugs drew my attention as I watched them in delight, remembering how I used to catch them in a jar as a child.

A half hour later, I went to bed. It was around ten that morning when Teresa came into the room, sat on the edge of the bed, and started bouncing up and down.

"Wake up, girl, wake up. Tell me about your date. I'm on mommy break. The girls are eating right now."

"Come on, Teresa, just give me another hour."

"No. Tell me everything, or I'll keep bouncing on the bed."

"Okay, okay. He was a good-looking brother. Let's see, bowlegged, and he had deep dimples. He likes to dance. You know about his son and that he's separated from his wife. I don't know if I want to get involved."

"Tell me why not, and please don't start that 'he's not Craig' shit."

"Just for your information, I didn't even think about Craig last night."

"What! I can't believe that," said Teresa with a smirk on her face.

"Well, don't. Anyway, this man is different from the other men. He had conversation that didn't include sex. He was mature, although I don't know how honest he was about his situation. He walked me to my car, and he didn't even try to kiss me. For all I know, he could be one of those married men who goes to the club to get the attention of other women, but knows where to draw the line."

"What do you mean?" Teresa asked. "'Cause you know my husband goes out on Fridays with the boys."

"Girl, get a grip. You know that man is not going anywhere. If there's a little flirting, it's innocent. Anyway, that's just it, he flirts, dances, gets a number, and probably never calls. We will see. I told him I was going away, and I'll call him when I get back."

"Okay, Cynthia, we will see. Go back to sleep. I better go check on the girls."

Just as I was about to close my eyes, my cell phone rang. It was Cole.

"Hello, Cynthia. It's Cole. Did I wake you?"

"No, I'm up. What's up with you?"

"Things got busy yesterday with the family, so I couldn't get away."

"It's okay. I went to the club last night."

"So you didn't sit and wait for my call?"

"No, I didn't."

"So, it's like that. You want to get together for lunch? I'm leaving this evening, and I want to see you again before I go."

"Okay. Why don't we meet around twelve thirty at Whaley's?"

Nothing was going to happen between us, but there was no reason why we couldn't share a meal before he left. Not every lost love has to become an enemy, and every encounter with and old boyfriend doesn't have to become a fling.

I got up, took a shower, and threw on some blue jeans and a light blue blouse. Teresa was still in the kitchen with the girls. She was washing dishes.

"Where are you going? I thought you were tired."

"I'm going to have lunch with Cole. He called when you left the room. He's leaving tonight, so we are just going to have lunch. Maybe we'll check out a movie after lunch. You mind if we reschedule our plans?"

"It's okay. Have fun. Call me when you get home."

Cole and I had a great afternoon. We didn't make it to the movies, so instead we decided to go on a picnic. We got a turkey sub, chips, and soda. We went to a nearby park, where we sat at a bench overlooking the water. It was nice. We spent hours just catching up with our lives apart from each other. We talked about our kids. We talked about our jobs and the picnic we had on his living room floor when I visited him.

When it was time for him to leave, Cole and I said goodbye once again. For a second time, there was a few hours where I didn't think about Craig.

The week was slow. Going to work and home were the gist of my days. I spent a lot of time on the phone with friends. I babysat for two of my work friends. One who went out for an anniversary dinner and the other for well-needed time away from their kids.

The weekend was here, and I was going to spend it with my grandchildren. This time I decided to go and visit with Kyle and his family. The weekend was great. I took them shopping and enjoyed the games I played with them (jacks, computer games, jump rope, and basketball). I taught my granddaughter how to make a few dishes for dinner and helped my grandson learn how to ride his bike.

When I got back from visiting with my grandchildren, I gave Barron a call. "Peace, Barron, it's Cynthia. We met at the club last Saturday."

"Hello, Cynthia, I remember you. What's up?"

"Well, I just got back in town from visiting my oldest son. What's up with you?"

"I'm here with my son. He's with me for the summer. We were getting ready to go out for dinner. I'm taking him to McDonald's. It's his favorite place. At least that's what he tells me."

"Okay. I'll let you go, and maybe I'll speak with you later in the week."

"You don't have to hang up just yet. I've been thinking about you. I thought about calling, but you said you would hit me up when you got back, so I waited."

"I was calling to see if you wanted to go out for dinner, but I see you have plans."

"Maybe I can get my sister to watch him later in the week, and we can do dinner then."

"I'll give you a call on Wednesday. I have to go now, my friend Teresa is at the door. Talk to you soon."

"I'll be waiting. Later."

Teresa and I went to the gym. After working out for about an hour, we went to the mall. We did a little window-shopping and bought sneakers for her girls.

On the way home, I got a call from Darren. "What's up, Darren?"

"I want to see you."

"I'm with my girlfriend right now. I'll call you later, and we can get together for dinner."

"Okay. Bye."

"Okay. Peace."

Teresa looked at me and shook her head. "Why are you messing with that man's head? You know he wants to be more than friends."

"I know, but what the hell, he's still good company. I'll make sure I reiterate the boundaries of our relationship."

Teresa stayed at my place for about an hour before she headed home. I gave Darren a call to let him know what time to expect me. When I got there, he wanted to take me to meet his sister. She lived around the corner from him, so we walked to her place. We had dinner there and talked about Darren when he was a lady's man. I'm still trying to picture that one.

When we got back to his place, he wanted to dance for me again.

"Darren, you know we are only friends. Dancing for me wouldn't be appropriate."

"Come on, Cynthia, I just want to show you my act. The last time we were interrupted, and I didn't get to perform my final scene. Please."

I guess he was still hoping to get lucky. I figured, *What the hell. If it would make him feel good, why not.* "Okay, Darren, go ahead and do your thing."

He put the music on and began to dance. By the time he was down to his boxers, he was at full attention. As I looked at him, all that ran across my mind was *Damn, he does not have anything over Craig or Cole.* It was time for me to get the hell up out of here.

I looked at my watch and said, "Damn, the time has gotten away from me, and I have to go. I have to pick my son up from work. I'm sorry, good show. I'll have to see if I can get you a gig somewhere. I had a nice time."

The next day, Craig and I got together. We cooked dinner together. We had crab cakes, mashed potatoes, and spinach. During dinner, I told him about my evening with Darren. After talking about Darren, I asked, "When are you going to introduce me to one of your friends?"

"It'll happen when it happens."

After dinner on the way home, we stopped and enjoyed a nice long walk along boater's row, strolling hand in hand. We took in the breeze of the summer's night air and the beauty of the crescent moon. We even talked about winning the lotto and moving to the West Coast, but we would still visit Philly every now and then. I knew not to take his words to heart.

That night, we made love. The more intimate we became, the more I could feel my love strengthen for him. His touch was so gentle, and looking into his brown eyes,

I felt a ray of warmth move through my body. It was as if my heart, which he had the moment I met him; my body, which I was finally able to give to him; and now my soul had found its home.

The next morning as I drove to work, with the excitement of last night still with me, all I could do was smile. I didn't care that he wasn't my man. I didn't care that he loved other women. I didn't care because I was in a place that I had never been, and it felt good.

Once I got to work, I gave Barron a call, as I had promised. But he was unable to go to dinner. He couldn't get his sister to babysit. We talked for a little bit, and he tried to make plans to meet another day for dinner. I told him we would keep in contact, and when the time was right, we would get together. We said our goodbyes. When I hung up, I knew that was the end of Barron.

For the next few days, Craig and I just spoke on the phone. I was missing him like crazy. One evening while I was soaking in a nice hot bubble bath surrounded by candles, a mixed CD of soft music in the DVD player, and a glass of white wine, I gave Craig a call. I asked him if he had a friend for me to meet yet.

After speaking with him for a few more minutes, he put someone on the phone. His name was Devon. Devon was a smooth talker. We spoke for about fifteen minutes, during which time we discussed going out to dinner. Before giving the phone back to Craig, I gave him my number. I hung up and gave Teresa a call.

"Peace, sister girl, you busy?"

"No. What's up?"

"I just got off the phone with Craig. He put one of his friends on the phone for me to speak with."

"Okay," she responded. "How did it go?"

"Well, first, there was the name exchange. His name is Devon. He's our age and has known Craig for six years. He said he wanted to meet me and suggested that we go out to dinner. I told him that would be nice and gave him my number. After that, he put Craig back on the phone. He was with the boys, so he said he'll give me a call tomorrow."

"Are you going to take this Devon up on his offer?"

"If he calls, I will go to dinner with him."

"Well, because this is a blind date, take him to a restaurant that is out of your zone. Somewhere that would require you getting on the highway. If things don't work out, when you get back on the road, you can lose him in traffic."

"Teresa, that's not necessary. Craig wouldn't introduce me to someone who would cause me harm."

"Fine, just call me when you go out, and let me know where you're going."

"If that makes you feel okay, I will. Go find your husband and have some fun. Later."

"I'll do just that. The kids are with their grandparents. Later."

Devon called the next day. We made plans to meet later in the evening for dinner. I suggested a restaurant called Antons, which was twenty minutes away from me. I must have gone through three outfits before I was satisfied with my attire for the date. I put my hair up in a bun and put on a pair of black sandals that strapped around my ankle to set off the outfit.

On the way to the restaurant, I called Teresa and told her where I was going. Then I gave Devon a call and told him what I was wearing so he would be able to identify his date. He was sitting at the bar when I arrived. He smiled as he walked toward me. He looked good. He had on a pair of navy blue slacks and a white shirt. He was about 5'9".

"Hi, I'm Devon, and you must be Cynthia?"

"Yes. It's nice to meet you."

"Shall we get a table?"

"Yes."

We walked over to the server and requested a table for two. She walked us to a table, and before sitting down, he pulled out my chair. He was a gentleman. Another server appeared and placed the menus on the table and then asked, "May I get you something to drink?"

"I'll have a draft beer."

"I'll have a white wine."

"Would you like to order now, or do you need more time?" asked the server.

"We'll need more time," replied Devon.

The server nodded and left.

"This is nice. Do you come here often?" Devon asked.

"I was here for a couple of events. Once was an outing with my coworkers and the other a baby shower for a close friend."

"Craig tells me you guys went to the same college."

"Yes." I began looking at the menu. "What are you having? I'm going to order the chicken Caesar salad."

"I'm going with the steak dinner."

The server returned, and we ordered our meals. Neither of us seemed to know what to say. Things just weren't really clicking with us. It was just a lot of small talk. There was silence for a few minutes, then Devon started talking about Craig. Where he met him at, how he taught him how to play pool, how he was like a big brother to him, and how he... He went on and on about this man. I worked with the conversation as best I could, but all he was doing was making me think about Craig.

When I noticed the server coming over with our food, I cut him off and said, "Food's coming." When the server left, I started the conversation this time.

"So, Devon, do you have any kids?"

"Yes. I have a daughter who lives down south with her mother. She's seventeen. What about you?"

"I have two boys and two grandchildren."

At this point, I was ready to go. We got through the rest of the evening talking about our kids. When the server came back and asked if we wanted dessert, I said no, and he replied with the same. We both knew that this date was going nowhere. He paid for the meal, and we left. He walked me to my car, and we exchanged the proverbial "It was nice meeting you," got in our respective cars, and headed home.

Teresa called that morning to ask how it went, and I just told her it was a date not worth talking about. Of course, when I saw Craig a few days later, I told him about our date. Yes, I tell him everything. After all, he did bring us together. Anyway, we were on our way to get his truck out the shop when I said, "Devon and I went out to dinner the other night."

"What? Why am I just hearing about this? The next time you go out with someone, let me know first. So how was the date?"

"He's very nice, but he spent the evening talking about you. He really admires you. We really didn't click. So until another prospect comes along, I hope we can still continue our relationship?"

He knew what I meant, so he just reached over, squeezed my thigh, and smiled at me. I smiled back and was glad to be spending time with him.

Chapter 28

The holidays were upon us again, and it was time for making New Year's resolutions. Hoping to end my search was mine, but so far, it wasn't going well, and my yearning for Craig was becoming stronger. The desire for more intimacy grew stronger, but also feelings of love became even deeper. I would think about him constantly. When I woke up in the morning and when I fell asleep at night. When I knew I was going to see him, I was still getting all excited. I wanted to make sure I looked good, and I was looking forward to the memories I knew we were going to share.

Three years had passed, and I still got butterflies in my stomach when he opened the door and I saw that handsome face. There's a momentary loss of breath, a weakness at the knees, and I would have to walk slowly just to keep from falling. I would even feel a little nervous. The nervousness arriving from the powerfulness I saw in him, which also gave off a sense of intimidation. All these emotions were turning me on to unbelievable heights.

There I was, forty-something, and feeling like a schoolgirl in love for the very first time.

I'm no longer looking for a true love because I have found it in Craig. He is what was missing in my life. We're different, yet we have so much in common. Enough was there between us for me to believe in us.

He still hadn't figured it out yet. I needed to get away again. I decided to take a trip to AC for the weekend. To be away from everything, free to relax and enjoy being me. I would put on my sexy lingerie and dance around in my room. Practicing for the day when I was ready to dance for Craig. I felt good, happy, and seductive. I could think about what being in love meant to me. That feeling you can't describe because it appears without warning. There are no red lights for stop, no yellow lights for slow down, or even green lights for go. The emotions bring immediate gratification that gives you instant joy, and all you can do is say, "Wow." You take a deep breath, you roll your eyes up to the top of your head, or you just close them to keep the tears from watering up in them. You become so overwhelmed with the emotions that you begin to analyze them, trying to figure out that one thing or moment you realized you fell in love. You look at the man who brings about this joy and happiness. You begin to realize what your life would have been like if you met him the moment you began your adult life. Would some or all your relationship trials have been eliminated?

Then it was that moment when you realized all this is because of you. It was a part of who you were, but it took this man to bring it to the surface. The creation of you is God. The right man being the one God has given to you. I say the right man because I have loved twice, and these feelings were never a part of those relationships. So you give him your heart because you're in love with him. Even a touch of submissiveness is there because it is what you want. A love filled with respect, honesty, and devotion.

Wow! What a revelation one can obtain from a weekend of solitude. By the way, did I mention I saw Kool & the Gang? They gave a nice show.

On my way home on Sunday, I gave Craig a call to see if I could see him. "Peace, Craig. I'm headed home from AC, and I would like to see you."

"Sure, I'm home. Come on by," he replied.

When I got there, we sat around and talked for a while. After about two hours, he asked if I wanted to take a ride with him to go pick his truck up from the auto repair shop. I was with him as a woman going to get her man and not to see her friend. It was a nice afternoon.

Later that evening, I went to see Teresa. We talked about Craig and how this time, although I said it a few times before, I was really going to make my move on him. She was really happy for me. The first thing she said was, "About time. You need to go for it and stop being scared. Don't worry about the other women. Just focus on the two of you."

"That's easier said than done."

"Well, if you keep worrying about them, you're never going to get what you want. You'll be the one miserable and lonely."

"I know, and I will try to, but I still have to guard my heart. Even though he already has it. I have to make sure he doesn't bruise it beyond repair."

Teresa called to her husband in another room to tell him I had decided to go after Craig—again. He came into the room, looked at me with a smile on his face, and said, "Do your thing and get that man."

I saw Craig again on Thursday. We went out to dinner to a very nice restaurant. After dinner, we went back to his place. He made some popcorn, put a movie on, and we cuddled together on the sofa. About a half hour into the movie, he dozed off. I laid my head on his chest and listened to his heartbeat with the love I had for him in my soul. I continued to watch the movie until I fell off to sleep.

That morning, we made love before I left for work.

Chapter 29

Today I had a mammogram that resulted in some findings. I was told there were calcium deposits in my right breast. I was told I needed to schedule an appointment with a surgeon to have a biopsy to determine if they were cancerous. When I got home that evening from work, I called Teresa and told her about my appointment. She comforted me with words of hope and said she would go with me to the doctors. The appointment was for the following week at which time my surgery was scheduled. When I saw Craig, I told him about it. He held me in his arms and said all will be okay. He asked me what they were going to do and I explained the procedure to him. It was referred to as a core biopsy and it would be two days before I would hear the results. I told him that Teresa and Robbie were going with me for the procedure. He told me to be sure to call him when I got home. He spent the rest of the evening making me laugh. He had always been good at making me laugh.

The procedure was on a Friday, so after it was done Robbie and I decided to go and see his brother. He thought that would keep me from thinking about the biopsy. I agreed, so I called Craig and told him I was going out of town for the weekend to see my grandchildren. He told me to take it easy, relax, don't be picking the kids, and to call and let him know how I was doing or if I needed to talk. Before hanging up, he told me to call him when I got there.

I saw Craig on Sunday, when I got back in town. He cooked dinner for me and listened to my fears about getting the results of the biopsy. I was getting ready to leave when he ask me if I wanted to stay. I guess he figured all I would do was go home and worry. One more thing I had come to love about Craig. He was really taking the time to get to know me. He cared about how I felt. Sometimes it felt like he could read my mind.

The doctor called Monday afternoon with the results, which weren't good. The test showed that they did not get the calcium deposits and she wanted me to wait thirty days for another biopsy procedure.

Thirty days later, I went in and had my second core biopsy, which also turned out to be unsuccessful. Whatever it was that she was aiming for wasn't producing the correct results.

Now she wanted to do it through surgery vs. the core procedure. I was becoming frustrated with this whole thing. I want to say "No," but I knew it was not in my best interest to fore go the surgery. All my friends were trying to assure me that everything would be okay, but I was still afraid.

This time a wire would be inserted into my right breast to help them identify the location of the deposits. I was assured that this was going to be a success. I called Craig crying on the phone about yet another failed biopsy. His words were kind but they were not easing my fear.

He finally said to me, "Stop crying baby girl, you're going to be okay."

"No I'm not. This will be the third time Craig."

Then all of a sudden, he starts singing to me. Before I knew it, I was smiling. His voice sound so soothing. Then I heard him say, "Come on up and see me."

I spent the night in his arms, which made me feel good, and for that day, that night, all was right with the world. When I got home the next day, I called Teresa and told her about my visit with the doctor. She was ready to come over but I told her I was fine and we would get together on the weekend. A few minutes after hanging up the phone rang again. It was a call for Robbie. He wasn't home, so I asked if I could take a message.

"Who will I be leaving a message with? Is this his sister?"

"No. This is his mother."

"You sound so young."

"Thank you and you are?"

"My name is Richard and your son is a friend of my sister. I wanted to talk to him about his music."

"Oh, I see. I will tell him you called. Does he have your number?"

"Let me leave it for him and you as well."

"I don't date anyone that is my son's age, but it's sweet of you to want to give me your number."

"I'm not his age. I'm in my forties. So, will you take my number and give me a call and will it be okay if I call you back soon?"

"Yes, you can give me a call."

"Okay. I'll call you soon and maybe we can have dinner."

"Okay. I'll let my son know you called. Later."

What was going on? Was I just flirting on the phone? Did I just make a date with someone? Yes I did. Now the question is will I actually go out with him? By the time I fell asleep it was 2:00 a.m.

That morning while enjoying a cup of coffee, I thought about what I was doing. I'm in love with my best friend, I'm thinking about going on a blind date, and I'm still married. My life with my husband was over so it was time for me to file for a divorce. I had seen him a few times after leaving and he was not making any changes with his life. Since I was off from work this week, it would be the best time to go and file paper for my divorce. The boys were grown so there would be no custody issues. He didn't have anything to fight for so it would be a simple filing. The papers would be served and as long as he didn't contest it, I just had to appear in front of a judge to dissolve the marriage. Within a month or so, I would be a free woman.

It was time for my third biopsy. Another trip to the hospital and another failed surgery. She wanted me to schedule another biopsy in six months. I called Craig and told him what happen.

"Peace Craig."

Before I could say anything else he asked, "Peace Baby. What's wrong?"

"I got the results back from the biopsy and she didn't get any of the deposits to test. I'm done. I'm not going through this again." I said to him with tears in my eyes.

"You can't give up. Are you going to the same doctor?"

"Yes."

"Then leave her and go get a second opinion. I'm with the boys right now. I'll call you a little later. Peace"

"Peace."

I did just that. She scheduled me that week. She did another mammogram and after looking at the previous films, discovered that, it was the moles on my breast. She actually brought the films in the office and viewed them while she looked at my breast. It was finally over.

Chapter 30

I finally got around to giving Richard a call. During our conversation, I found out he lived in Lake Placid, New York. He invited me up for the weekend after I told him how I hadn't been to New York in years. He said he would put me up in a hotel. After talking it over with Teresa, I decided to go. We had a very nice time during this visit. We caught a movie, went out to dinner, and went dancing. We had some things in common. Even though there was a controlling side about him, which I didn't care for, I decided I would give him a chance.

Darren couldn't excite me enough to become a partner, but could exist as a friend. Cole was no longer part of that search since he was married. I blew that the first time Cole and I met with the choice I made to stay with my husband. Barron and I couldn't get together because he always had his son. Devon, well, he never made it to first base. Craig and I were growing closer to each other, but there was no commitment at this time. I was prepared to take the next best thing.

I saw Richard as one last chance to see if there was someone who could pull my heart away from Craig. Someone who could offer me what I was getting from him with a little more consistency.

In the meantime, the good news that did come my way was that my estranged husband was served the divorce petition. Robert called when he got the papers to see if it was what I wanted. I told him yes, and he said he wouldn't contest the divorce.

As I moved on about my day, I received a call from Richard. "Hey, Cindy, what are you doing this weekend?"

"Well, Mother's Day is this Sunday, and the only plans I have is going out to dinner with my son."

"I would like to see you. I can come there, or you can come here."

"I would like to come there. Let me check and see what time dinner is so I can make sure I am back in time. I'll call you tomorrow to let you know what time I will head up on Friday."

"Okay. I can't wait to see you. I had so much fun the last time we were together."

"I have to go. Stay sexy." I could hear him saying yes before the receiver hit the cradle.

It was another nice weekend. We went on a horse and buggy ride. We went to a club, and one night he even cooked dinner for me. It was a pasta dish. The only thing missing was the feeling I got when Craig cooked for me. It wasn't there with Richard. It was nice, but it just didn't have that passionate feeling. I stood in the kitchen and watched Richard cook as I sipped on a glass of wine. My eyes saw Richard, but my heart was feeling Craig. Then I realized why. There was playfulness with Craig, and he wanted me to help him. I was in charge of the little stuff while he handled the main dish for the meal. It was a shared moment.

So I went to help Richard, but he didn't want me in the kitchen. So the fantasy of cooking together wasn't there. He didn't even want me to set the table. While he was trying to impress me, he was taking away the connection that I would have liked in sharing the task with him. With Richard, it was niceness vs. togetherness. When you are always doing something alone, when you're with your love, you just want to do things together. For me that enhances the memories. I know I have to give it a chance. That it isn't fair for me to compare the men I meet to Craig. He has my heart, so no one will compare anyway. I have to learn how to accept them for who they are, but a girl wants what a girl wants.

I called Craig on Wednesday to see if we could get together.

"Peace, my love."

"Peace, baby. What's up?"

"I want to see you."

"I'm around. Come on up."

"What about something for dinner?"

"How about picking up some soul food from Delilah's at the train station?"

"That sounds good. See you soon."

When I got there, I put the food on plates while he got the drinks, napkins, and silverware. See, that's what

I'm talking about, working together as a couple. Later we shared dessert while watching a movie. Movie night was always nice. We would watch the movie together while I laid my head on his chest or cuddled in his arms, and before long, he would fall to sleep. I would just smile and shake my head. In the morning, I would tell him about the rest of the movie he missed.

Who was I kidding? No one was going to make me feel as good as Craig was making me feel. It was time for a talk with Teresa. I hadn't seen or spoken to her in a week or so. She and her family had gone on vacation. Actually, it was one of those "get all the ladies together" night. We went to dinner at Red Lobster. As always, each of us would tell what was going on in our lives since the last time we met.

Teresa told us about her vacation in Florida. She passed around pictures of their vacation. Jackie informed us that she was expecting, and of course, we all started screaming. Jackie and her husband were definitely back on track and no longer thinking about a divorce. I told them about my weekend with Richard.

Teresa was the first to ask, "Okay, did you tell Craig about Richard?"

"No. I didn't tell Craig about Richard." I had finally told the girls about Craig after we became intimate.

"Okay, Cynthia. Tell us why you not? You told him about the other men you met."

"I decided that Craig didn't need to know." The playing ground was different now that I decided I wanted to take our relationship in a different direction. When I decided that I wanted to pursue Craig. Anyway, the first couple of visits with Richard were nice, but the time together wasn't giving me the feelings I got being with Craig. The visits, however, were a lot more exciting than the ones I had with Darren. Still, no one gave enough to hold my attention for long.

"Did you sleep with him?" asked Jackie.

"No, and before you ask, he didn't turn me on enough to want to jump his bones at first sight."

"So, are you going to see him again?" asked Jackie.

"No, she's not," Teresa replied. "Cynthia, why are you wasting your time when you know he is not going to live up to Craig's standards? During your time with Richard, did you find yourself comparing his every move to Craig?"

"Look, ladies. I'm done looking at other men. I decided last night that Craig is it. I am going to devote my time to Craig. See where it goes. I thought Richard would have been a possibility, but he wasn't. As Teresa said, no one will be able to fill Craig's shoes. I was going to settle for someone close, but I have been settling all my life. I'm not doing that anymore. I love me some Craig. No other man will ever do."

"You go get your man, Cindy. I'm with you all the way. You have been playing around with this far too long," said Jackie.

"Okay, not to change the topic of conversation, but my divorce hearing is in a few days. Robert and I will be no more."

"We will be there for moral support," said Marsha.

"That won't be necessary. It's just a formality."

We all had one more toast before heading home. We toasted to Jackie's pregnancy, my divorce, and for me to go after my one and only true love, Craig.

On the day of my divorce hearing, I woke up with the feeling that this was going to be the best day of my life. I was doing what was right and best for me. I was going back to my maiden name. When the hearing was over, I called Craig and shared the news with him. Craig came up for a visit, and we celebrated, even though I didn't have my divorce decree in my hand.

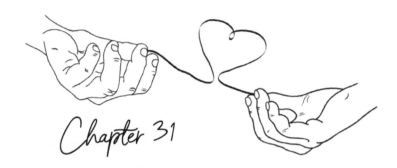

Chapter 31

It was my forty-fifth birthday, and the girls wanted to take me out to dinner. I told Craig, and he said we would do something soon. It was a fun-filled night. After dinner, we went to the club. This was the first time we all went together. Jackie and Marsha stayed on the dance floor. We all flirted the entire night, including Teresa. On the way home, we made a pact. Whatever happened at the club, stayed at the club.

That following week, Craig and I went to a bar over in Jersey. They were having a barbecue out back, so we sat out there. He introduced me to a few of his friends. He walked around talking to people, but always made sure he wasn't gone too long and that I was okay. At one point, I went off to the ladies' room without telling him. When he found me on my way back to the table, he was a little upset.

"Don't you ever walk away without telling me where you are going. Understood?"

"Yes. I only went to the ladies' room."

"Just say something the next time."

After that, we continued to enjoy the evening. The memory that sticks out the most about that night was singing a song by the artist Lenny Williams called "'Cause I Love You" on the way home.

Two weeks later, on Friday, I received my divorce decree in the mail. What a great weekend gift. I called Craig and told him I was holding my divorce papers in my hands.

"Now we really need to celebrate," he said.

"Yes. What do you want to do?"

"I'll come up later, and we will go to dinner."

"Okay. I'll talk to you then. Peace, honey."

"Peace."

I called the girls and gave them the news. We all got together on Saturday to celebrate at Teresa's house. Teresa bought me a picture frame for my decree. Marsha brought the champagne. Jackie brought a seafood pasta dish she made. Even Rochelle showed up with a trophy inscribed with "I'm Divorced." Rochelle was always the happiest about my leaving Robert because she knew him and always regretted introducing us. She wanted me to let him go the night of the club chaos that took place shortly after Robert and I got together.

I think I did a little too much celebrating because I woke up Sunday morning with a hangover. Craig called about an hour later. During our conversation, we decided to go out to brunch. I met him at a spot in south Philly. As soon as he saw me, he told me how nice I looked. It was a nice little restaurant, and we had a view of the street, so of course we talked about the people who walked by. There was even some foot playing under the table as we laughed and talked about everything, but nothing.

He had something to do later, so after brunch, I returned home. Before I pulled off, he kissed me, and then he said, "I like the color on your nails." It was a champagne color.

Since it was early, I went to spend the day with Teresa. We took the girls to the movies.

A few days had passed, and I was yearning to be with Craig. So I gave him a call.

"Peace, my love."

"Peace, baby. What's up?"

"My love for you, that's what's up."

"That's nice to know."

"I want to see you."

"I'm down at the beach."

"Who are you at the beach with?"

"Don't worry about who I'm with."

A statement like that generally meant that you were with a woman. So why did he answer the phone when I called? Anyway, we went ahead and talked for a few minutes as we normally did (laughing and singing little melodies). Then all of a sudden, he had to go. Guess that meant she was returning to be with him.

Alone as usual, I thought about my relationship, and I began to cry. It wasn't because I was sad; it was because I was thinking about the things he had done that touched my heart and brought about my love for him. They were tears of joy. I usually only got those feelings when I sat around looking at photos of my boys as I took a walk down memory lane. There's nothing or no one who could tell me that this man is not the one for me. I am so whipped. Even when Teresa and I talk about him, she could see the love I had for him in my eyes. She said they sparkled. Isn't a love worth having worth fighting for? I believe that it is.

I spoke with Craig a few days later when he returned from the beach. We talked about us, my love for him, and how he perceives that love. Then the subject of sex came up. "When are we going to make love, baby girl?" he asked.

"Didn't you just give my love to another woman?"

"What is her name?"

"I don't know because you never told me."

"When was this?"

"It was while you were at the beach."

"Did I tell you I was with a woman?"

"No."

"What did I say to you?"

"Don't worry about who I'm with."

"Not that I owe you an explanation, but I was with one of my boys. I allowed you to let your imagination run wild because it was apparently what you wanted when you asked me who I was with."

I forgot how he hated to be questioned and that generally, when he wanted me to know something, he would tell me. We hung up a little while later, but not before hearing him say, "Watch your imagination. It could be a downfall to us. I've got to go, my boy is at the door, and we're going out for a while."

"Okay. Peace, baby."

"Peace."

He called me the next morning on my ride to work, which was nice. We spoke a few more minutes, but before we hung up, I told him I loved him, and he told me that he loved me too. I smiled all day long.

On Sunday, the girls got together, and we went to Jackie's daughter's baptism. Yes, Jackie had a baby girl. The event was very nice, and the sermon was about going back to your first love, that being God. That to him belong all of your trust, your commitment, and your devotion.

I saw Craig that following Tuesday. As always, I had a very nice time with him. I stopped at the market on the way there and picked up some chicken. He prepared a meal of grilled chicken, corn on the cob, and asparagus. We also had cherries and strawberries for dessert and some Moët. He even gave me a gift that night. It was a very nice watch. I asked him what it was for, and he said, "Just because I love you." He is the sweetest man in the world, and I love him with everything that I am.

I thought about him all day and how much I enjoyed being with him last night. Where has this man been all my life? Why wasn't I taken by him when we were in college? Well, it was better late than never. All that mattered now was that we were getting closer.

It was time to see where we really were. I saw Craig a few days later. During this visit, I decided to ask Craig if he was going to introduce me to someone else. I was going to tell him that he didn't have to and that I wanted to explore more of a relationship with him. I was ready to humble myself to him. So standing in the living room in a pair of well-fitted color jeans (down to a size 7 from a

12 when I first reconnected with him), looking out on his deck, I asked, "Craig, are you going to introduce me to any more of your friends?"

"I am not," he replied. "I'm keeping you for myself."

Well, that was all that needed to be said. Those six words were enough for me. We spent the rest of the year just enjoying the relationship. I saw him two to three days a week. I loved him more and more each day. He began sending me sweet, passionate, and romantic text messages. Loving him was just as easy and wonderful as it was being with him. When we weren't together, I missed him as much as I loved him. Yes! We were in a relationship. It was about time, and I am so glad I didn't give up on us.

I think about all the things that he does when I am with him that keeps my love growing. I think about the ways that he touches my heart. From the moment I hear his voice on the phone, my heart begins to fill with a sense of warmth just knowing that he is on the other end of the call. Our conversations can be short or long. On the occasions when I ask to see him and the answer is no, I feel sad at that very moment, but before we move on to something else, he starts singing to me and the joy returns instantly. I am putty in his hands once again.

It was during this time that I began telling Craig about my family. He helped give me a better perspective on them. He told me how I needed to let things go and to be thankful that my mother didn't abort me. So one day, I decided to go and visit my sister. I gave her a call, and we talked for a few days before I made plans to go over. During one of our conversations, she mentioned that she needed to get her hair done. I told her one of my friends could do her hair. She said okay, and I told her I would call and see what day was good for her.

I informed Craig of my plans to visit my sister. He told me to call when I was in town. When we got there, my mother was there hoping to get her hair done as well. It would take her four hours to do their hair. I needed to find something to do, so I called Craig to see if he wanted to go out to dinner. He was free and said yes. I asked him to pick me up at my sister's and that I wanted him to meet her. Introductions went well, and we left for dinner.

The next day I spoke with my mother, and she asked me if I was looking to replace my ex-husband with Craig. She thought they were similar in appearance. They were both tall and slim-built with close haircuts. I simply told her no and that Craig was a better man than my ex-husband could ever be.

As I mentioned earlier, there has only been one other man who I had this sort of connection with, and that was my oldest son's father, Randall. Although we were young and our relationship short-lived, the first time I laid my eyes on him, he took my breath way. There were no orgasms, but an attraction nonetheless. Yes, the relationship ended when I got pregnant, but the feelings stayed for years. Now I have Craig, and I have never been happier.

Four years had passed since Craig and I met, and within the last year, we were getting closer. We made plans to take our first trip together. It would be an overnight trip to celebrate my birthday. We went to the beach in Wildwood, New Jersey. He had the time that we would spend together all planned. My ex-husband never planned any of our trips. It felt good to be with someone who did all the planning, and all I had to do was just follow his lead. I knew that I could trust that he would treat me with the utmost respect and wouldn't do anything that would bring harm to either of us.

We arrived there at about the same time (2:15 p.m.) and began the day by going to the beach. He sat on the bed and watched as I put on my bathing suit. It was a green one-piece with a tank top that gave it the appearance of a two-piece suit. He thought it was a nice suit. Before going to the beach, we stopped at his car to get a blanket, pillows, sweaters, something to drink, and his radio. He even brought some sweet Jersey corn. I went to one of the shops on the boardwalk and got us a turkey sub. I also bought some sunblock and a swimming cap.

The time we spent there was very nice. We were in and out of the water. We laughed, talked, and spent time in silence as we listened to the news on the radio when we weren't listening to music. He mentioned to me that he had gotten me something for my birthday, but he forgot it at home. He would give it to me the next time I came up.

We left the beach at around 7:00 p.m. Back at the motel, we took a shower together and made love before going out to dinner. We went to a seafood restaurant where we sat out on the deck and enjoyed dinner (laughing and talking about his recent trip to Rome). He was very affectionate at dinner, and I just felt like I was in heaven.

After dinner, we went and sat on the boardwalk for a little bit, and he told me about the history of the boardwalk and why he thought men were dressing in that baggy clothes fashion. He felt it came from the way the prisoners dressed, and it became a fashion statement for the youth.

We went back to the motel, got undressed, and relaxed for the remainder of the evening. He even turned off his cell phone, and I had his undivided attention. He went to sleep, and I watched him from time to time and realized how much I truly loved this man. I got up out of bed and got down on my knees and thanked God for him. I finally fell off to sleep, but not without the thought of us making love yet again. We did at around 4:30 a.m.

Later that morning, at around 7:45 a.m., a wonderful trip ended. Now I'm left with memories to last until we meet again.

When I told Teresa about my time with him at the beach, she was so happy for me. When I told my sister, she responded by saying, "You know he does this for his other women." I didn't care, nor did I bother to ask her why she even thought he had other women. I was *happy*.

Chapter 32

We began to have conversations about my days at work, tales of my family, and friends. The best part was that he listened to me. Never once had he said, "I don't want to hear about that shit."

He complimented me often, told good jokes, and just listened when that was all that was required. I still find it hard to believe that I had found such a man. As each day passed, I found him to be a wonderful blessing. There was more passion and pleasure than I could have ever imagined. Years had passed, and his voice was still intoxicating. He was still singing sweet little melodies to me and telling me that he loved me. Now don't get me wrong, things are good, but he does do things that can irritate me. His ego can get the best of you, and he can be a bit overbearing, but it doesn't tip the scales to all that is good.

The next time we got together, we went out to breakfast and then bowling. We talked about me looking for a new job. I was ready for a change. The following day, I forwarded my résumé to a professional recruiter company. They sent me on interview three weeks later, and I got the job. On my first day there, Craig sent me some beautiful flowers.

The first week on the new job was great. The people were nice, and my staff were knowledgeable in their positions, so I was able to focus on what I needed to do to keep the office running smoothly.

It was girls' night out, and we decided to get together at Teresa's place. I went straight from work. Everyone was doing fine. Jackie asked, "Have you set an anniversary date to acknowledge the turn of your relationship with Craig?"

"No." After answering Jackie, I did make a mental note to discuss it with Craig on our next visit.

"Ladies, tonight we will not talk about our men. Tonight we are going to do each other's nails, watch a girlie movie, and pig out on junk food. We all have love in our lives, so tonight belongs to us," said Teresa.

We had a good time. We had so much fun that we decided to turn it into a sleepover. I left around four the next afternoon to get ready for a dinner date I had with Craig. I had on a cute backless black dress. At dinner, I mentioned us having an anniversary date to celebrate the union of our relationship.

"Okay, Cindy, pick a date for us to discuss."

"I think it should be around the time you decided we were close enough to be in a relationship."

"When was that?"

"During a conversation we had back in January, you mentioned that we had been close for a year. Which means that we have been in our relationship for a year and a half as of today. I would like to make it January 5."

"That's fine with me."

So there you have it. The obstacles that were there seemed to have disappeared. We are in the midst of planning our next vacation to Las Vegas. I was caring for him in every way that matters. My dreams and prayers were answered. My blessing from God had come. I had a wonderful man whom I intended on spending the rest of my life loving. We became inseparable. "You for me and me for you." Those were the words often said that I based our relationship on. God, I pray to you for wisdom as Craig and I get to know each other. Guide us through this journey of love, and help us come closer to you. Amen.